NECKING
WITH LOUISE

Rick
Book

Red Deer Press

The Publishers
Red Deer Press
813 MacKimmie Library Tower
2500 University Drive NW
Calgary Alberta Canada T2N 1N4
www.reddeerpress.com

Credits
Edited by Peter Carver
Cover photo by Tony Stone Images
Cover design by Dean Allen / Cardigan.com
Text design by Dennis Johnson
Printed and bound in Canada by Webcom Limited
for Red Deer Press

Acknowledgments
Financial support provided by the Canada Council, the Department of
Canadian Heritage and the Alberta Foundation for the Arts, a benefi-
ciary of the Lottery Fund of the Government of Alberta.

THE CANADA COUNCIL | LE CONSEIL DES ARTS
FOR THE ARTS | DU CANADA
SINCE 1957 | DEPUIS 1957

National Library of Canada Cataloguing in Publication Data
Book, Rick.
Necking with Louise
ISBN 0-88995-194-2
I. Title. II. Series.
PS8553.O636N42 1999 jC813'.54 C99-910090-4
PZ7.B64495Ne 1999

5 4 3 2

NECKING
WITH LOUISE

Rick
Book

To Mom & Dad

Contents

NECKING
WITH LOUISE

The Clodhopper's
Halloween Ball

"So," said Dad, hesitating like he was straining to haul the words up from some well, "you're goin' on your first date tonight."

Jeez. I looked out the windshield. We were driving past my Uncle George's slough, heading up to a field to pick rocks. I could tell Dad had to make some kind of speech. I kept my eyes on the road ahead.

"Well, I can't believe you're old enough." Dad glanced over. I felt my face grow hot. I didn't know whether I was embarrassed for me or Dad or both of us. I hoped this wasn't about sex or something. He'd never talked to me about that. And this wasn't exactly the time as far as I was concerned.

"You know how we feel about Anna-Maria. She's like a daughter . . ."

I tuned him out like a radio station you can't quite get, like the ones that come skipping in across the prairies at night from Omaha or Kansas City, that fade in and out through the static. So I was going to the Halloween Sock Hop at the high school with Anna-Maria. Big deal! I'd known Anna-Maria since grade five, when her family moved to Lashburg. She's Italian. Her big brother Domenic's a couple of years older than us, a great baseball and hockey player. Renaldo and Theresa, her parents, are best friends with Mom and Dad. Renaldo owns the hardware store in Lashburg and was in the Italian Resistance during the war. He's a nice enough guy—a little moody because of the things he's seen, I guess. Theresa's different, full of fun, always laughing, an incredible cook. She taught Mom how to make pasta from scratch. Which is not something people in Saskatchewan know much about, even though we grow the durum wheat that's used to make it.

Dad cleared a load of gravel out of his throat like he does when he's tense. *Don't let this be The Big Talk.* I figured God already knew about that party at Peter Bourin's place when we were in grade seven. I'd stayed overnight in town with friends. Someone pulled beer for us and we had a gallon jug of Calona wine, real cheap stuff. We joked about whether it would work better as paint remover or panty remover. Brave talk. Peter's parents were away. We all got pretty tight drinking beer and wine and snarfing all the chips and dip we could, and then everyone got down on the linoleum floor and started playing Spin the Bottle. I got Margaret Handle once—she's cute—and then Liver Lips Davies, the undertaker's daughter, picked me. You wonder how a girl can have such awful tasting lips. It's not as though you can brush them with toothpaste or anything. Anyway, that got the party going.

Later we were all dancing away to "Love Potion Number Nine" when people started disappearing. I saw Bev Bradley go into a bedroom just off the living room and I followed her in. The lights were out and there was a lot of giggling going on and I could tell someone was in the bed. Bev yelled, "Slide over!" and climbed in and I jumped in right behind her. Brian and Dorothy and Peter and Gayle were already there, but they sure weren't taking up much room. When I got in, Bev turned around and we started kissing. Just like that! You could hardly move, and we were hot and sweaty under the flannel sheets and blankets, and we just kissed and groped away. I finally got up the nerve to touch her right boob and she let me keep my hand there. They were huge, but I already knew that from watching her play sports at school. That's why we called her B.B. She thought for a long time it was because of her initials. She was madder than a wet cat when she found out. Anyway, they sure were soft. I was kneading them through her blouse and that industrial strength bra of hers. After a while I started to undo her buttons. But she whispered, "No," and that's about as far as I got. After about an hour of necking, we all came up for air and piled out to the kitchen for more food and beer. That party was good for about two years' worth of talk, and the best thing of all was, Bev was a year older than me and in grade eight, so I felt like that was really something special.

Dad drove our new Chev half-ton into the field and we bounced across the ruts. We were headed for some big rocks he'd turned up summer-fallowing. Dad's getting up there, about 42, I think. Not exactly the life of the party, but he plays catch with me a lot, baseball or football, and sometimes he comes out and plays hockey with us on the slough. He was smoking a cigarillo (rum-soaked, wine-dipped) and wearing one of his HOP-X grasshopper spray hats. I'd noticed lately he had bits of gray in his hair. Farming isn't exactly an easy life.

Dad stopped the truck next to a boulder. It was still buried, just the round, white top sticking out like some dinosaur egg. Wouldn't that be something! We got out, got the crowbars and spades out of the back. Dad was thin compared to most of the farmers I knew who generally got fattened up on their wives' home cooking. He jammed the crowbar into the ground beside the rock, stopped, took the cigarillo out of his mouth and horked a gob of spit down into the dirt. I looked at the foamy green and brown blob floating there in a dusty crater of its own making and thought that there could very well be life on Mars. Dad looked at me, kind of fiercely, I thought. Turned out he wasn't finished with his speech yet.

"I just hope you always behave like a gentleman when you're out."

Sometimes parents can be so damn serious. Like they know you're going to do something wrong or bad and they always want to give you advice. I just wished they'd lighten up a little and leave me alone. As far as I was concerned, I was too much of a gentleman. I was afraid Anna-Maria thought I was boring. Trouble was, I was just a big farm boy, nothing special to look at. I wanted to be more like James Dean or Elvis Presley—or a Beatle, even. Someone who could really make moms and dads worry. I guess when I stop and think about it, what I really wanted to be was dangerous.

Anna-Maria and her family came out to our farm all the time, and she and Domenic and my two sisters used to play shadow tag or hide and seek at night. And as we got older, we hung out at school a lot, skated together at the rink, stuff like that. That's about all you had to do to be girl friend and boyfriend in a small town like Lashburg. And with only about 500 people, not counting dogs and cats, you didn't have much choice anyway.

The first time I ever kissed her was in grade eight. We were driving around one night with about twelve kids crammed into Lenny Roberts' mom's '61 Chrysler and we were sitting two-deep and four across in the back seat. Anna-Maria ended up in my lap. There was no room so she had to bend over toward me, with her head close to mine and, well, we were tearing along Elevator Road when we hit this

15

The Clodhopper's Halloween Ball

bump and Anna-Maria's head bounced into the ceiling.

"Oooh," she cried and kind of collapsed onto my shoulder. I put my hand on her head—to feel if there was a bump. She turned and smiled at me and we kissed. Everyone else was too packed in to notice, so we did it again. Just soft and gentle-like. Then Anna-Maria lay her head on my shoulder. We both knew right there that we really were much more than friends, and from then on I didn't feel like we were kids anymore, either.

We kept driving around and laughing and telling jokes, and we went back past the elevators because we didn't have anything better to do or anywhere better to go, for that matter. We saw my best friend's car parked next to the grain buyer's office beside the United Grain Growers' elevator. And I thought that was funny because Peter was probably necking with Gayle and he picked the elevator his dad hauls wheat to. Is that a habit or lack of imagination? And if it's lack of imagination, I wondered how far he was getting with Gayle. My dad belonged to the Saskatchewan Wheat Pool, so I thought Anna-Maria and I better go there sometime. I laughed at my little joke, but it made me think about Dad and me and the farm and where I would end up some day. Certainly not in Lashburg. I knew that.

It was Anna-Maria who answered the door when I showed up that night. "Oh shit," she said, laughing. Which I thought was a hell of a way to greet a guy on his first date. Her head was covered in fat pink rollers and she was in a scraggly, beige terry cloth robe.

"I'm a little late." She shrugged and rolled her eyes as if to say, *You know me.* "Domenic's watching the hockey game, Dad's down in his workshop and Mom's in the kitchen. Go on in." She laughed again and ran upstairs. Her laugh made me think of wind chimes.

Any nervousness I had about this being a first official

date just kind of fizzled away. It was more like I was coming to pick up my favorite sexy cousin or something. I
walked down the hallway to the kitchen, where Theresa was
standing over a huge aluminum pot on the stove, the biggest
pot I'd ever seen. The steam clouds rising out of it were in
danger of producing garlic rain.

"Hiya, Eric," she cried and gave me one of her famous
Italian-Momma–type hugs and I kissed her once on each
cheek like she'd told us Italians in Italy do. "I'ma making
some-a pasta sauce. Maybe I send some home for you-a
Momma."

I nodded. "Sure, that'd be great." Next to Mom, Theresa
was the best cook I'd ever known. We never got tired of
spaghetti, especially with hot and spicy sauce when it was really cold and blizzarding outside. "Looks like a spaghetti night,"
we'd say, and Mom would head to the basement to get one of
the jars of pasta sauce she'd made. And we'd have that with
garlic butter on her hot-from-the-oven homemade bread.

"Here, what d'ya think?" Theresa dipped a big wooden
spoon into the bubbling sauce and held it out to me. "Careful, it's-a very hot."

Of course it was wonderful. Theresa had me wrapped
around her finger. It wasn't just her cooking. It was because
she and her family are Italian, from Europe, where they have
statues and homes that are a thousand years old and churches with masterpieces on the ceilings. I'd never been out of
Saskatchewan, except on a holiday to British Columbia last
year with my family, and once to Edmonton to a football
game. So she and Renaldo were different, kind of exotic, in
a *National Geographic* kind of way.

"Mom, you stuffin' that guy again?" Domenic came
around the corner from the living room. "Come on, leave him
alone. He's goin' dancin'; he don' wanna eat." He nodded at
me and we escaped into the living room to watch the game.

"I put some-a sauce by the door," Theresa called after us. "You canna get it later when you bring Anna-Maria home."

The Black Hawks and Red Wings were playing. The game was boring until Delvecchio got slashed and a huge brawl broke out. And right in the middle of it, there was a voice at the doorway.

"Okay, I'm ready." Anna-Maria was standing there, hands on her hips. Golly! She looked like a picture from a magazine. Her blonde hair was all puffed out and she had a black band in it like the ones Annette Funicello wears in the movies. She was wearing a black, V-neck sweater, jeans and black sneakers.

"So?" She snapped her fingers and stood there, green eyes flashing, pretending to pout. I got the message.

"Groovy." I meant it. She looked . . . well . . . sophisticated. Almost. A cross between Sophia Loren and a cat burglar. It made me proud, but it made me kind of nervous at the same time. I hoped I didn't have cow shit on my running shoes.

"Let's get going," I said with one last glance at the TV, where they were picking up gloves and sticks from the ice.

Our high school's an ugly pile of boxes, not exactly a design that inspired higher learning. A couple of teachers and our principal were at the door checking for bottles, trying to get close enough to smell if we had lemon gin or cherry brandy on our breath.

"Look at ol' Wild Bill Brylcream," Anna-Maria said. Our principal, Bill Keen, was bald as a billiard ball and famous for his wrinkled ties and soup-stained shirts with buttons missing just above the belt so you could see hair from his pot belly. He was patting down some of the guys wearing jackets.

"Jeez, he can't do that," I said. "The guy needs a search warrant."

"Hiya, Mr. Keen." We sailed right by with hardly a trace of snarkiness. I turned and saw him checking out Anna-Maria pretty close. He wasn't looking for hidden bottles, either.

The gym was decorated with orange and black streamers, witches and black cats on the wall. It was dark as a barn, except on the stage where a disk jockey played records, surrounded by jack-o'-lanterns with fiery, lopsided grins. In front of the stage, silhouettes danced as the Rolling Stones sang, "I Can't Get No Satisfaction."

Anna-Maria grabbed my hand and pulled. "Come on." We joined Peter and Gayle, Brian, Margaret and the rest of the gang. I liked that she just started right into dancing because it usually took me a long time to get my nerve up. Anna-Maria was a good dancer; girls just are, I guess. I'd watched *Dance Party* on TV after school, but I never felt like I knew what I was doing. Everyone was watching everyone else, so we all ended up dancing pretty much the same way, anyway.

The DJ put on "My Girl." "Great, a slow one." I grabbed Anna-Maria's hand. Even in the dark she was pretty. Maybe it helped that she was always laughing. Even her eyes laughed.

"I just thought of something," I said, stepping carefully, waiting to see if she was curious.

"Yeah? What?"

"I never thought of it before, but how come you're blonde? I thought Italians all had dark hair."

"Oh, you think this is a dye job?" Anna-Maria teased.

"No-o-o, I just wanted to know, that's all."

"We're from northern Italy, near the Po River. A lot of people there are blonde. Couple of my aunts have red hair, too."

"Must be something in the water, eh?"

She laughed.

"Or maybe those Vikings got farther south than we knew." I was Norwegian and liked having marauding sea-farers' blood in my veins, even if we were clodhopper dirt farmers stranded thousands of miles from the sea.

"Maybe we're distant cousins?" There was mischief in Anna-Maria's voice.

"Uh-huh, kissing cousins at least." I kissed her then, on her cheek, right in front of her right ear. Right in front of Bruce "The Goose" Longstaff, too. He was our own Icha-bod Crane of an English teacher. But he just smiled in that lonely way of his. I tightened my arms around Anna-Maria and she pressed herself closer. The heat of her body, the feel of her cheek against mine, her two legs moving against either side of my right leg, perfume, spaghetti sauce, garlic. I was swimming in a pool of it all.

"Hey, you two!" Peter called from ten feet away. "Song's over, guys." Which I took as a sign that the date was going just fine.

"Wanna Coke?" I was feeling kind of dry.

"Orange Crush."

We went to the back of the gym, where a table had been set up. Our student council was selling stuff to raise money for the yearbook. Liver Lips was sitting behind the table with Tess, a real brainer who looked the part: thick glasses, mousy stringy hair and a tiny little mouth that almost hid her buck teeth. A real tire biter, as the guys would say.

We chatted with them a bit. Tess had read that the Bea-tles might be going to Toronto for a concert in Maple Leaf Gardens.

"Oh, wouldn't that be incredible!" Anna-Maria was already fantasizing about that.

"I, on the other hand," I said, "would go to the Gardens if I could see the Canadiens beat the stuffing out of the

Leafs. The Beatles would make a good show between periods, though."

Anna-Maria laughed. "Imagine, them riding around on the Zamboni singing 'Help!'" She squealed at her own joke.

"Speaking of *help*—" Liver Lips stopped and leaned forward in a gossipy sort of way.

"Yeah, what?" Anna-Maria took the bait like a hungry pickerel.

"You heard about Dennis Funk and Ginny McIntyre?"

"No, what happened?" The DJ was playing a new song: "The Birds and the Bees."

Tess joined in. "They were caught out in a field east of town." She paused to set the hook. "They were doing it!" Her eyes lit up like Christmas morning.

"You're kidding?" I said. These people were old and married—and not to each other. Dennis and Shirley were friends of Mom and Dad. They'd been out to the farm just weeks ago.

"No! It's true!" Tess was enjoying being in on something other than the right answer in math class. She looked at me. "Your cousin, Ken, found them."

Holy shit. This kind of thing doesn't happen in Lashburg. The big city maybe, but not here. What's going to happen to Shirley, and Ginny's husband, Boris? Word must be spreading like prairie fire.

"Ken found them doing it in the field?" I needed to double-check.

"In their car, yeah. Apparently ol' Dennis was so hot and bothered he had his foot on the brake and, of course, that meant the taillight was on—so to speak." Liver Lips snickered. "Ken was driving by and thought somebody was stuck and needed help."

"Stuck all right," Anna-Maria laughed. We all yucked it up at that one.

"He shone his flashlight in," Liver Lips chimed in. "He said they looked like two badgers cornered in a barn."

I felt sick about it. Like the time Sigurd Christiansen caught his leg in his tractor's power take-off and almost died. Their lives were ruined, I knew that. They had kids in school. They'd have to move. And here we were, laughing and trading one-liners about it like hockey cards.

"Come on," I said to Anna-Maria. "Let's blow this place." I grabbed her hand and tried to head for the door. But she held back.

"No, wait," she said. "One more dance." She gave me a sucky smile. "Please," she said, tilting her head to one side like it was a big favor.

Ian and Sylvia were singing, "You Were On My Mind." All I could think of was two people, old as my parents, for crying out loud, screwing out in the field under the stars. Why'd they sneak around like that? Were they miserable? Were they in love? Were they just plain horny? What the hell were they thinking of anyway? "Hey," said Anna-Maria. "You're squeezing my hand awfully tight, you know."

I was angry at them. I felt nervous. The witches and cats on the walls of the gym seemed so stupid now. The smiles of the jack-o'-lanterns had turned into burning, sordid leers. Dancing seemed crazy and pointless. There was something mysterious and powerful about it all, and it was much bigger than I could understand. And it scared the hell out of me.

"Penny for your thoughts." Anna-Maria had pulled back to look at me.

I laughed. I really wanted to go somewhere and talk and hold Anna-Maria. The song ended.

"Can't dance but I can sure intermission," I said, forcing another laugh. "Let's go for a drive."

We hopped in my '58 Ford and drove down the main drag toward the CNR station. There wasn't a soul on the street. Just the taillights and a trail of dust from a lone car.

We passed the Red & White grocery store, Dean's BA service station, Milt's pool hall, the Canadian Imperial Bank of Commerce with its gold letters, the Lashburg Credit Union—a low brick box of a building—Renaldo's hardware with its pressed tin siding, Hank's grocery store, the Chinese café that closed last year, a couple of little grandmother's houses and that was about it. Many of the buildings had false fronts like in western movies. I'd never noticed before how old and shabby and small they looked. The Supremes were singing "Stop! In the Name of Love" as we circled around town and headed toward the railway crossing by the elevators.

"Want to walk along the tracks?" I asked, stopping by the crossing.

"Sure, I've never done that."

"Never! How come?" Secretly, I was glad.

"Too scared, I guess. What if a train comes by?"

"Not much chance of that these days. Besides, you'd hear them out here."

We got out and walked to the wooden planks on the crossing between the tracks. A cold north wind cut across the stubble fields. It had already snowed once but only a skiff that hadn't lasted more than a day. Winter wasn't far off, though. Coal-black clumps of clouds skidded across the sky, obliterating stars and the half moon. I did up the snaps on my hockey jacket. "You warm enough?"

"Uh-huh." Anna-Maria leaned into me and scrunched up her shoulders. She was wearing her high school jacket and a Cowichan Indian sweater underneath. Girls were always cold, I'd noticed. But at least Anna-Maria wasn't admitting it right now. I gave her full marks for that.

We turned and walked along the ties. The crested wheat grass that grew alongside the gravel railway bed was dry and brittle. The ties were black with creosote and the smell reminded me of Indians fishing from bridges up north. The tracks were silver streaks in the dark.

"It's amazing when you think about it, eh? Our wheat goes out on these all the way through the Rockies to Vancouver. Or east to Thunder Bay or Churchill."

"So why were you so upset when they told us about Dennis and Ginny?"

Anna-Maria's question took me by surprise. I turned to look at her. She was ready, her eyes looking hard at me. I felt a warmth pour through me like hot chocolate after a game. Anna-Maria cared about what I thought. She knew something was wrong.

"Your parents aren't going to split, are they?"

"No," I laughed, a bit quickly. "I don't think so, anyway." I paused. "They still hold hands and have afternoon naps on Sundays."

Anna-Maria laughed.

"How about yours?"

"Oh, they're okay, I guess." Even in the dark I could see Anna-Maria's face go into a pout like it did when she was conjugating irregular French verbs. "They're so different. I wonder why they even got married sometimes. But I think they love each other—in their own way."

We were moving slowly, my arm around Anna-Maria. She snuggled in close. We took short steps as we walked along the ties.

"Mom and Dad had a big fight the other day. I don't even know what about. Money, maybe." I hesitated a minute, then said it. "I unplugged the distributor cable on the car so he wouldn't take off, like he always does."

Anna-Maria looked surprised. Then she laughed. "Yeah, mine fight about money, too. And stupid things. Mom likes to throw things. They just need to blow off steam."

I thought of Mom and Dad's wedding pictures. They

had looked so young and happy. "I dunno. People fall in love, get married, have kids—and then they have to work hard and they get old and . . ." I paused. "It seems like parents just settle. What happens to the love?"

Anna-Maria stopped. "Dennis and Ginny didn't settle, did they?" She turned to me. "I wonder what will happen to us, don't you?"

I'll never forget the way she looked, standing there shivering in the dark and the cold, the wind blowing her hair, her face so serious, so beautiful. I'd never been so warm in my life. And right then all I wanted to do was fold her into me, right inside me until she felt warm and safe and protected and loved. I put my hand under her chin, raised it and kissed her. A long slow gentle kiss that tried to tell her about all the strange and powerful feelings that were in me. A kiss like never before.

"Mmm," she sighed, smiling sweetly. "I think we'll have fun finding out." And then Anna-Maria turned, stepped up on one steel rail and held out her hand to me. Laughing, like wind chimes. I stepped up on the other and we held hands and walked, each balancing on our own rail. We walked westward, away from the small scattered lights of town, toward the mountains and the sea beyond.

The Game

LASHBURG TIGERS		
FORWARDS		
Left Wing	*Center*	*Right Wing*
1 Murray 17	Bryan 11	Eric 9
2 Mark 12	Roddy 27	Cam 19
3 Dana 18	Allan 15	Mike 14
DEFENSE		
1 Daryl 6		Tony 3
2 Dennis 7		Peter 5
3 Trevor 2		Jim 4
GOALIE		
Gerry 1		

THE COLD SCISSORED away at my clothes, poked with steely blades through zippers and down my collar. The sky was a piercing blue, not a cloud in it. Snow sparkled fiercely, so much it hurt my eyes. A snowshoe rabbit started and ran, white disappearing into white. I'd had to get out of the house. I was walking to the Tree Patch Corner, a square of trees my grandfather had planted a half-mile south of the farm in the hope a son would live there some day. Clouds of steam from my breath, blown like a horse before a race. Leather glove pounded into leather. Not to keep warm. Tonight was the big game. I was getting ready.

★　★　★

"And playing right wing, Nummmberrrr Niiiiinnne . . ."

The crowd drowned out my name as I stepped onto the ice, legs like two Slinkies. The voices of a thousand farmers roared, filling the Lashburg Ice Palace with a happy riot of sound. One by one we skated between two rows of the Lion's Club Marching Band, past honking tubas and squawking trumpets and beer bellies straining at white shirts. Cameras flashed like lightning. Cowbells clattered through the crowd. Trevor and Bryan and Daryl and the rest of the Lashburg Tigers were at our blue line. We banged each other's shin pads, punched each other's helmets. "Let's go, guys! Let's get 'em!"

This was the championship game against the Rousseau Rockets, the third game of a best-of-three final. The winners would be Midget champs of the whole province. I looked around. Everyone I had ever known was here and a few hundred more I didn't. *Jeez*.

The voice of the announcer crackled out of the public address speakers. The band struck up a half-frozen facsimile of the national anthem. With knees locked, I tried to focus on the game ahead. Rousseau had beaten us in the first game a week ago. Three nights later, we had won in over-time with a deflected shot from the point. We'd been lucky. On the other blue line, the Rousseau boys were lined up like crows on a dead tree. They were almost all bigger than us. And faster. And, as a matter of fact, they were better, too. But we'd been playing with heart. I looked over at our coach, Tilt McCann. True to form, he'd had a nip or two and was leaning at a precarious angle. In the dressing room Tilt had said the team that wanted to win most would be the winners. His Three Feathers Whiskey words splashed over me like gas on a fire. Nobody wanted to win more than me.

The anthem was over. The crowd was testing the workmanship on the roof. They should have known better. Most of them had built it. The farmers in this hockey-mad town had made sure that the ice in our new rink was one inch longer than the ice at Maple Leaf Gardens. It's amazing how much bigger that inch made us feel. Our member of parliament headed out to center ice with his shiny three-piece suit, black hair slicked sideways over his bald spot like seaweed on a rock. He dropped the ceremonial puck. The crowd roared again. The band marched off. The referee signaled to the goal judges at each end, then blew his whistle. We were ready.

I lined up on right wing. Murray at left, Bryan center, my cousin Daryl on defense with Tony. Gerry scraped back and forth across his crease like a caged cat. The Rousseau left-winger across the center line from me snarled. There was a zit convention in full swing on his face.

Tilt had said something else in the dressing room. A scout was in the crowd tonight. An NHL scout. He was looking for players to send to Junior B teams. I felt like I'd grabbed an electric fence. This could mean a trip to the Saskatoon Blades, the Regina Pats and then a farm team and then—the NHL. To *Hockey Night in Canada*. To sweaty, between-period interviews with Ward Cornell. "Well, I'd just like to say hi to the folks at home in Lashburg."

The ref dropped the puck.

Necking with Louise

★   ★   ★

It had seemed like an old game already when I was little. I remember my Uncle George pulling it out of a battered cardboard box with end flaps ragged as a stray dog's ear. It had shiny red plastic sides and a varnished plywood surface that rose up in the middle at center ice and slanted down toward the goals at each end. The players were simple wooden pins, red or green, like clothespins with bent wire hockey sticks. And when you pulled the single looped-metal handle at your end of the game, all your players moved at once. The goalie was a wooden peg, too, guarding a wire frame net with a crocheted mesh. A stainless steel ball bearing for a puck.

We played it on Christmas Day and New Year's Day when Dad's side of the family got together. The women with their new red dresses and big aprons were in the kitchen, hot and steamy and fragrant with turkey, mashed potatoes, pies and perfume. The men would stand or sit around in the living room in tight suits and too-tight ties, peeling the labels off Red Cap Ale or Pilsner Lager as they talked. Some would roll cigarettes, reaching into shiny cans for tobacco, sprinkling it into flimsy papers. Rolling with one hand and then a lick, a twist and a flick of a lighter. Later, when the ashes got too long, they'd tap them into pant cuffs or empty beer bottles. Grandpa and Grandma would be there, too, sitting with old friends on the couch, admiring every new doll and cap gun and sweater their grandchildren presented. And all I ever wanted to do was play that hockey game. With Dad, with my cousins or with Uncle George and his big farmer sausage fingers and Buster Keaton face. I fired the ball bearing with the pinball launcher. I pulled and my players whirled and passed and shot until my finger got a blister, until the blister broke, and I pulled some more until the Band-Aid wore off and the supply of adult opponents wore out.

★   ★   ★

Rousseau won the draw. The puck went back to the defense, a pass over to right wing. Three of them came over our blue line, a drop pass to defense, a shot. It hit Daryl and fell in front of him. He looked up and saw Bryan busting over our blue line, headed for center ice. Daryl floated a pass two feet off the ice. But the Rousseau defenseman had seen it coming. He reached out, caught the puck, dropped it, skated in, and took a slap shot. It ricocheted off Tony's skate, past Gerry into the corner of the net. It had taken thirty-two seconds. The quiet fell like an ax. Tilt was roaring.

"What the hell's the matter with you guys? Get off the ice." The second line jumped over the boards. We sat in shame, checking the scoreboard, shocked to see that number 1 in lights under Visitors. "You wingers, you gotta pick up your man at the blue line. Don't let 'em walk into the circle like that. Make the buggers shoot. Christ Almighty." Whiskey fumes vaporizing.

The second line did better. They had Rousseau cooped up in their end for the whole shift. The crowd came alive again with cowbells and tambourines and trumpets. The puck came out to center, and our third line jumped over the boards. But Rousseau stole the puck and fired it into our end. Peter went into the corner to get it, the Rousseau left-winger poked at his feet with his stick. Peter fell. A thousand referees called for a penalty. No hand went up. Rousseau fired the puck into the slot. Their big center was waiting. He one-timed it into the top right-hand corner, over Gerry's shoulder. The red light went on. Two–nothing. Five minutes into the first period. This wasn't the way it was supposed to work out.

*   *   *

"Here you go, son." Dad, just home from town, put the parcel on the table. It was wrapped in brown paper with an Eaton's label.

"Go ahead," said Mom. I tore it open. Inside was a cardboard box with a red and blue picture on the top. A hockey player in full flight, all his weight on his front leg, stick back, shooting, scoring a goal maybe. I opened the box slowly, enjoying the promise of that picture. The sharp smell of new leather. A nest of white paper. Shiny black, shiny brown leather. Not a mark on them. CCM stamped on the back. The blades glistened. I ran my thumb across the edge. They were sharp. I uncoiled the shiny yellow laces, thick and stiff with wax, and threaded them into the skates.

"Thanks," I said, hardly able to look up.

There was no snow. But there'd been a melt and then a freeze because the puddle in front of our front steps was frozen. Mom and Dad went into another room. I went out and sat on the steps, and put on my skates. They fit perfectly. I tied the extra lace around my ankles twice. Round and round I went on the tiny rink. The door opened. Mom and Dad stood there, laughing. They'd wondered where I'd gone. I was just outside pretending to be the guy on the box.

*   *   *

A hand on my shoulder pad. Tilt leaned over. "I'm counting on you," he said. "Now get out there." I turned, surprised. It was the first time Tilt had given me a compliment, had given me a mission. I jumped over the boards. The face-off was in our end. The puck went back to Peter on defense. He circled behind the net, looking to pass, but Murray on left wing was covered. Two Rousseau players charged in and slammed him into the boards. The puck slid free. I raced over and grabbed it behind the net, stopped, turned and headed back up right wing to our blue line. A quick pass to Bryan at center. Back to me. Over their blue line. Their left defenseman was backing up fast. I deked left and he went for it. I put on a burst of speed and leaned, turning around him, keeping the puck well out and tucked in my stick. The second Rousseau defenseman came across to block me as I tried to cut in the front of the net. Bryan had fallen. I couldn't see Murray. I leapt over the second defenseman's stick, pushed the puck between his legs. I wheeled around him, grabbed the puck again. Their goalie slid across the crease, and then went down, a wall of leather trying to block my backhand. I took another step, waited, then flipped the puck over the goalie. CLANG! It hit the crossbar and flew up over the net. The crowd roared. The red light flickered but stayed off. The ref waved his arms to the sides, palms down. No goal. The crowd booed. But it didn't matter. I'd done something I'd never done before. And I knew something else—I would do it again. I wondered where Mom and Dad were. The scout was forgotten.

★   ★   ★

Our old prairie rink had been a dark and fragrant place. The beams had aged to the color of tea, the hockey boards black with the memory of a million shots. In the waiting room, the wooden floor was reduced to slivers by generations of blades. Two skate-nicked wooden benches lined the walls and another went down the middle. There was a big-bellied, coal-wood stove with an iron ring around it hung with drying mittens. And always the smell of burnt wool and woodsmoke and coal. The hockey ice was built next to the curling ice with an open walkway between and a bench for watching either side. Mom and Dad often curled in the regular draw on weeknights. I was there for the public skating. We played tag and crack the whip to scratchy records of "The Skaters' Waltz" and "Chattenooga Choochoo." Old Mr. Wilkie, our rink caretaker, in his ragged cardigan sweater and cloth cap, always pretended to be cranky. But after skating, a few of us would help him clean the ice with heavy iron scrapers. We'd bring the snow to the end of the rink and Mr. Wilkie would shovel it outside through a small wooden door. Then he'd turn the lights out, lock up and go home. The town kids would go home, too, and I had the rink all to myself. My hockey stick and puck had been stashed and ready.

Light spilled over from the curling rink, the beams casting shadows across the ice. Skating from light to dark, dark to light, blades flashing like bayonets, white sprays of snow arcing out with each stride, the sound of steel cutting ice, the sound of rubber on wood, breath like a locomotive in the clean cold air, the boom of "a cannonading drive" echoing in the darkness. I took a pass from Doug Harvey, stickhandled around some Maple Leaf, made a brilliant pass to Rocket Richard. He shoots! He scores! We basked in the roar of the Montreal Forum. Danny Gallivan called it "a scintillating play." A rink rat alone in his glorious palace with only the pretty McDonald tobacco girl on the scoreboard watching.

★   ★   ★

Our line was sitting together on the bench. "Guys," said Bryan, breathing hard after our shift. "I think that big Number 10 on defense is hurt. He's awful slow. If we make quick passes we can beat him."

Bryan was a favorite of my Dad's. "Hardest working guy on the team," he said. Meaning I wasn't.

"We gotta be first into the corners," Murray added, then

looked at Bryan. "Remember what we worked on last practice? We'll get it to you behind the net, then the other winger can get into the slot for your pass."

I just nodded. It felt strange, like we were in a movie. It was real but at the same time it wasn't. It was like being in overdrive, yet everything was in slow motion. Somehow I knew we were going to win even though we were down. I felt something I'd never felt before in my life. It was power. It was weird.

Tilt cursed. "Damn it all to hell!" We looked up. We had a penalty. For two minutes Rousseau bombarded us with rubber. But we held them off. Our line was back on. Bryan picked the pocket of the Rousseau centerman and shot the puck into their corner. He looked at me. I knew what to do. I raced in. The Rousseau defenseman heard me coming and braced for a body check, but I ignored him, swatted the puck free from his skates, and shot it behind the net. Bryan was waiting. He took a step to the left side of the net, stopped, went to the right and fired the puck through the crease out into the slot. The pass was perfect, right on Murray's stick. He shot. A quick wrist shot, right between the goalie's pads. The red light triggered a storm of sound. Murray was mobbed. Sticks high, smiles big. The Lashburg Tigers were finally on the scoreboard. We were on our way.

★　★　★

We called it George's Slough. A huge pond beside the road next to my Uncle George's and Aunt Margie's farm. It was full of pickerel weed and cattails. There were plenty of ducks, and blackbirds sang in the gnarly willows that grew out of the rock pile at one end. In spring we'd go rafting there and catch frogs. In winter it was our hockey rink. On Saturdays, after a morning game in town, I'd call my cousins Jim and Barry, who lived on the farm next door. And we'd walk up the road for a game of shinny. First we'd have to clean the ice. We'd made scrapers out of plywood with a strip of iron bolted along the bottom. When the snow was too deep or too crusty, we had to use wheat shovels first. We worked up a sweat long before we ever got our skates on. It was never warm, sometimes twenty or thirty below. And by the time the ice was clear, our skates would be frozen so we'd light wooden matches and hold them inside. It took three or four to warm up the toes enough. We played for hours and hours, calling the play by play as we went, each rush a different player.

"And now Bobby Hull, the Golden Jet, winds up behind his net. He's driving down the ice, blond hair flying. A slap shot—"

"Ohhh! Ol' Scarface, Terry Sawchuk, makes an incredible save! And the crowd roars. . . ."

We used our boots or chunks of snow as nets. And when the new arena was built in town, I got the old nets. The netting had rotted, so I bought some chicken wire and lashed it onto the frames with binder twine. We felt pretty special, having real, regulation-sized hockey nets. Often we'd lose the puck in the snowbank and spend half an hour digging with sticks and shovels trying to find it. Sometimes Dad would come out to play, and once I remember George put on his skates. George and another uncle, Babe, had played semipro hockey in the States during the thirties. Dad said they got paid fifty cents for playing a game on New Year's Day in Los Angeles in 1933.

Margie would wave from her kitchen window and George would invite us in for a bowl of soup and a sandwich. And lots of cookies, of course. They never had any kids of their own. After we'd petted their old black collie, Major, for a while, we'd go back out and play until long after dark, and only when we couldn't see, we'd get into our cold boots and walk home soaking wet, skates and sticks slung over our shoulders, talking hockey, looking forward to the game on TV that night.

★   ★   ★

Our hopes were shortlived. With two minutes to go in the first period, the snarly Rousseau left-winger got a breakaway. He deked the shorts off Gerry. We went to the dressing room down three to one.

A few fathers came in. They stopped in front of their sons to drop a word or two of advice. A big boot nudged my shin pad. I looked up. It was Dad. "You guys got to pass more, like you did on that goal," he said. I could tell he was pleased.

The door opened. Tilt lurched into the room, his face as red as ours. We knew he'd gone to the can for refreshments from the mickey he carried in his coat. "Gentlemen," he said to the fathers, "I need a few minutes with my boys." Tilt waited while they filed out. The room grew quiet. Tilt blinked, trying to focus his mind and perhaps his eyes, too.

"Nerves," he said in a surprisingly quiet voice. "You guys were just nervous." He stood in the middle of a square of faces with wet hair plastered and rivers of sweat running down eyes, necks. "Now that you've got that out of your systems, you can go out there and get back to your game." He paused, looked around. "The game that got us here." Another pause. "Or was all that hard work this year just for nothing?" The question floated like a balloon held up with heavy breathing. "That's all I gotta say," said Tilt.

★   ★   ★

Scamp barked. Dad looked out the kitchen window. "Marty's here." Marty was one of my favorite uncles. He was a great hockey player. I'd seen him beat a goalie once with a slap shot from center ice. He opened the door and walked in, wearing a shit-faced grin. We all laughed. He had a turkey under his arm. A live one.

"Here you go, Bart and Donna," he said to Mom and Dad. "Here's your Thanksgiving dinner." The turkey must not have liked the sound of that, for he squirmed to get a wing free, but Marty just squeezed his arm a little tighter like he was playing the bagpipes.

"Where'd you get that?" asked Dad, still laughing.

"Turkey shoot." With his free hand, Marty grabbed a wooden match from the wall holder by the fridge and started chewing on it.

"Why don't you want it?" asked Mom, suspicion lurking in her voice like a cat in the weeds. She was his older sister, after all.

"Can't kill it," said Marty. "Thought maybe you could."

"Okay," said Dad slowly, as if a free bird wasn't much of a bargain at all. He turned to me. "Maybe you can take it out to the chicken coop for now till we figure out what to do with it."

The turkey's head shot around and he looked at me, folds of skin dangling from his beak all wrinkled and red like an old farmer's neck. I grabbed his two legs and tucked him under my arm. "Think I'll call him Henry," I said. The three of them laughed.

Henry never did become Thanksgiving dinner. We let him roam around the farm, and one day I was shooting a rubber ball against the barn with my hockey stick when Henry ran after the ball. He ran it down like Eddie Shack and gave it a good peck. After that Henry played shinny with me whenever I was outside, even in the snow. Of course, being a turkey, he was a Toronto Maple Leaf. I'd stickhandle around him, Henry trying to peck the ball, then I'd shoot it in the net and Henry'd gobble and run into the net to get it. He didn't know about goals. When it got cold

Henry moved into the barn and survived Christmas without so much as a glance in his direction about dinner, even though we thought nothing of chopping the heads off chickens or putting a .303 bullet into the brain of a cow at butchering time. But one night the next spring, Henry just disappeared. We think he may have been drafted by a pack of coyotes. By that time my hockey-playing turkey had become the talk of the family and luckily we had the photos in the album to prove it, just in case *Ripley's Believe It or Not* ever came by.

★   ★   ★

We came out of that dressing room hungry as traveling salesmen in a bad crop year. For the first couple of shifts we buzzed around Rousseau like flies on a cow pie. We made quick little passes, then shot the puck in and raced into the corners. The bigger Rousseau guys were faster on the straightaway, but we were better in close. We forechecked like crazy, badgering them into making bad passes. But for ten minutes neither side came close.

Then Murray intercepted a pass. He raced down the left boards. I raced down at center, Bryan close behind. One guy back. Murray cut to center drew the defenseman and goalie with him across to the right of the net, whirled around, made a backhand pass to the front of the crease. The empty net was open as a barn door. I drilled the puck into the twine. Bryan right behind me had his stick in the air before the goal judge had the light on. The crowd went nuts. Three–two.

The Rousseau boys were rattled. You could see it in their faces, in their rushed passes, in the way their coach started juggling lines. They weren't used to losing control of the game. We had momentum.

Five minutes went by. Rousseau started throwing their

weight around, using their size to slow us down. Dennis, on defense, never saw it coming. He put his head down to stop a puck along our boards. As he did, one of their big right-wingers came charging in, lined him up and—BAM— bodychecked him into the boards. It was a clean hit. But there was a post there that held up the heavy wire mesh that protected the crowd in that end. Dennis's head hit the post his helmet flew off. At the same time, the butt end of the Rousseau winger's stick came up and sliced a smile across Dennis's left cheekbone. He grabbed his face and dropped like a heart-shot buck. Blood splashed on the ice. The good thing was he was still moving. Tilt came running with a towel.

Dennis went off to the dressing room to a standing ova-tion—most people were standing anyway. The PA announc-er called for Doc Drummond or Doc Peters, the local vet. One of them would have to get his black bag out of the car and do some sewing.

If Rousseau thought that would slow us down, they were wrong. They'd just swatted a bull on the ass and now we were mad.

★   ★   ★

When you grow up in a place like Lashburg, you just think every other place is the same. And it surprises you when it isn't. We almost always played league games somewhere else on Saturdays. Dad and the other fathers would have carloads of kids and we'd crawl up the highway to a distant town along the railway line through near-blizzards, drifting snow, or sparkling thirty-five below days. Once we pulled into a one-horse town and found the rink locked and no other team in sight. Dad eventually found the caretaker—in the beer parlor. When he flushed the guy out, and he'd grudg-ingly unlocked the door, we walked into the world's largest refrigerator. There was no heat on, no fire in any stoves in the waiting room or dressing rooms. Some people might have turned around and gone home. But we never gave it a thought. We just got wood, shoveled some coal and lit the stoves—in record time. In our dressing room the caretaker had kindly left the frozen hose he'd used to flood the ice. It was writhing all over the floor like a big black snake with a severe case of rigor mortis. There was a plywood door in the dressing room that opened into the toilet—a two-holer nailed onto the side of the rink. There were ice crystals in various shades of yellow around the ragged rim of the ply-wood seats. And even frozen solid, the stench would have made a magpie puke. We felt sorry for the kids in that town. But it made us want to beat them even more. And when they finally rounded up their team, we did.

★   ★   ★

With a man advantage, our second line got quick revenge. Cam simply decked one of their left-wingers with an elbow he never saw. The ref didn't either. Gordie Howe would have been proud. The Rousseau player crawled off the ice on his hands and knees and the crowd yelled for more. Then Roddy, our center, picked up a pass from Peter in our end, and swept by their centerman. As he crossed their blue line, Roddy slowed. Mark, his left-winger, barged ahead through the defense like a bowling ball, cre-ating all kinds of chaos, screening the goalie. Roddy let fly with a low wrist shot through a forest of legs. The first time their goalie saw the puck was when the ref fished it out of the net. Tie game.

The Rousseau boys came back. For the next five min-utes we skated end to end, making plays, trading shots, goalies sprawling to make saves. Then Rousseau's center on their first line picked up a rebound in front of his net. He

fired it up to his right-winger. Their left-winger took off
like a cut cat. A long pass over to him. He crossed the blue
line, passed it back to the centerman. And that guy did
something I'd never seen before. Just as Trevor moved to
swat the puck away from him, the guy let the puck slide
from his stick back into his skates. Trevor lunged for it,
missed it. The Rousseau center kicked the puck out to the
left with his skate. He breezed by Trevor like he was standing still, surprise and panic on his face. Jim, the other
defense, moved up to stop him, leaving the Rousseau left-
winger alone on Gerry's doorstep. Bang. The centerman
passed it over. Bang. The left-winger knocked it in. Gerry
went down—half a second too late. It was a pretty goal. It
was four–three. That's the way the period ended.

★   ★   ★

Fresh asphalt and pine were my two favorite smells in
the world. It meant we were almost at Waskesiu. "Whiskey
Slough," Prince Albert National Park, a five-hour drive
from our farm into the lakes and rocks and trees of Canadian Shield. Every summer, we became refugees from the heat
that seared our dryland farm. We'd come up in July, when
the fields were still lush with promise, and we'd often return
two weeks later to find the crops burnt to a crisp, hope
shriveled, and dreams put off for another year. Waskesiu was
our green oasis.

Our car was loaded and so was the white speedboat on
the trailer behind—tents, sleeping bags, cooking gear, water
skis and fishing rods. My sisters and I'd strain to be the first
to spot the park gate, the lake, the golf course and then the
town itself. It was like rolling into a prairie Disneyland with
its painted cabins, the brown log museum with the stuffed
buffalo inside, the velvet lawn bowling greens, tennis players in their whites. And Johnny's Café.

Dad pointed it out as we drove by. "There it is." I had expected it to be all lit up with flashing lights and big signs. But it was a simple little building with clapboard siding, yellow with white trim, just like Grandma's house. A faded wooden screen door with a Coca Cola handle. And the sign, Johnny's Café. Through the window, a glimpse of people at the counter.

"Why don't you go in later and get his autograph?" said Mom as we drove on to our campsite. "After we get the tents set up."

Forty-five minutes later I pushed through the door. Palms sweaty, stomach tight, mouth dry as August. I walked to the shiny old cash register at the end of the counter. A skinny blonde girl with a very dark tan and very red lips was smoking a cigarette and fiddling with the radio dial. She turned when she saw me, took another drag.

"Hiya." She didn't inhale. "What can I do for you?" She smiled, friendly, not much older than me but miles ahead.

"Is J-J-Johnny Bower here? I'd like to . . . ah . . . like to get his autograph." *Stupid farm kid*. That was probably what she was thinking.

"Sure thing," she said. "Just a sec." She wheeled around and walked to the back, through swinging doors with round steamy windows.

The Toronto Maple Leaf goalie was wearing a white T-shirt, whitish pants and a dirty apron that he wiped his hands on as he walked alongside the counter toward me.

"Hi kid, how are ya?" said Johnny Bower, the guy I'd watched for years on TV, mostly on a snowy black-and-white TV.

He's shorter than Dad, I thought. *And almost bald.*

"Hi, Mister Bower." Swallow. "I wonder . . . could I have your autograph?" I couldn't take my eyes off his face. It was like it had been made out of rubber and left out in the sun too long. And while it was melting someone had come along with a sharp stick and drawn all these lines on it. I could even see little dots where some of the stitches had been.

"Sure . . . got an autograph book?" I shook my head. "No problem." He bent down under the counter and pulled out a paper place mat with flowers on one corner. "This do?" he asked. I nodded.

Johnny reached down into the pocket of his apron for a ballpoint pen next to the yellow receipt pad. "What's your name, kid?"

"Er . . . Er . . . ic." Johnny put the place mat on the counter, leaned over, pen hovering. "You play hockey?"

"Yup." A gulp. A swallow. A nod of the head. "Right wing. For Lashburg."

Johnny nodded. His pen swirled over the paper like a skater. Miss Lipstick was back, adjusting her hair in the mirror behind the milk-shake glasses.

There was a sign on the counter: Today's Special—Hot Turkey Sandwich. *Henry!* And then panic! *What if he asks me my favorite team?*

"There you go, Eric." He looked up. "So, who's your favorite team?"

A slap shot to the gut.

"Uhhh, Canadiens."

Johnny's head jerked; he straightened up. "Canadiens!" he said. Three men at the far end of the counter turned. Miss Lipstick gave me a scornful look. And then Johnny Bower threw back his head and laughed. A big deep laugh. "So, I suppose you like that Jacques Plante guy, eh?" I cracked a smile, nodded, picked up the place mat in case he changed his mind.

"Thank you very much," I said. "I think you're great, too." I wanted to make a run for the door.

He laughed some more, winked at Miss Lipstick, then reached out and swallowed my hand in his. "No problem. Come back for breakfast anytime, kid." He turned and headed back to the kitchen. I ran to the door. I took about a week to recover, and then I went back, once, ate bacon and eggs and toast real slowly, but the NHL's second greatest goaltender wasn't there.

★   ★   ★

Third period. Rousseau came out flying. They came at us wave after wave. They outskated us. They outpassed us. They outsmarted us. The only thing they couldn't do was beat Gerry. And even he wasn't invincible.

Rousseau's defenseman picked up the puck in front of his net. A pass over to right wing. The guy turned, sidestepped Mark, who tried to deck him. Over to center. The left-winger was heading for our blue line, a pass to him. He raced for the corner, turned to go around behind our net. Dennis, with eight fresh new stitches, went in after him, looking for revenge. Bang! Into the boards. Missed him. The guy carried the puck around to the other corner, the crowd yelling, "Nail 'em! Get 'em!" A pass back to the point. A slap shot. It hit Gerry in the chest. He never saw it. The rebound out in front. Four sticks flailed the air. Four bodies wrestled together. The puck between their skates just sat there. Rousseau's left defenseman snuck in like he was late for church, blasted the puck at the corner of the net. Gerry dove for it. The puck bounced off his trapper and trickled into the net. Gerry lay face down on the ice, defeated. Dennis stood with his chin resting on the end of his stick, shoulders slumped, cut oozing blood. Cam dug the puck out of the mesh and fired it down the ice. The busload or two of Rousseau fans tried to fill the rink with sound. It didn't work. It didn't matter. The scoreboard told the tale: five–three.

Our fans were quiet. Our bench was quiet. Tilt was strangely quiet, too. The game was slipping away like snow-drifts in April. The puck went back into our end. It was always there now. Jim on defense tried a clearing pass. It hit the Rousseau left-winger's leg and bounced right in front of him. He stepped between Jim and Trevor and drilled a shot past Gerry's stick side. A loud groan. The scoreboard lights changed again: Home 3, Visitors 6. There was movement in the crowd. Questions. Shrugs. A few people shuffled off for coffee. They'd never think of leaving.

★   ★   ★

Daahdadada, daahdadadadahh. Canada's unofficial national anthem was playing on TV. Saturday night and it was blizzarding outside. In the kitchen there were small muffled explosions. Mom and my sisters were making pop-corn. Dad and I were getting ready, too. The towel was laid across the dining room table, the hockey game on top so we wouldn't scratch the wood. The game was brand new from Christmas. It had batteries and real red lights behind each goal. There was a separate rod for every player, so every play-er could move up and down the ice. You could stickhandle by twirling the players back and forth. And every player, made of pressed metal, had a face. It was Toronto against Montreal on TV. It was me against Dad at home. The bowl of popcorn with melted butter and salt arrived. And glasses of Coca Cola. Mom stayed in the kitchen reading recipes. My sisters took their bowl up to their room and played. Murray Westgate stood by the Esso pumps. He saluted, like an uncle, waving. The girls on TV were singing, "The Esso sign of confidence, the happy motoring sign." Every kid knew the words.

Danny Gallivan: "Hello, sports fans from coast to coast, it's *Hockey Night In Canada.*" Ward Cornell was there in his chunky dark suit and black Brylcream hair. He talked about the rivalry between the Leafs and Canadiens. Dad and I had our own going. I'd never won a game. But each time, I got a little closer. Before the game on TV began, we'd start. We played between each period. And if necessary we played after the TV game was over.

Now it was time. I sprawled on the floor, raised up on my elbows, to watch my Canadiens. Here in the middle of the prairies, on a farm in the middle of nowhere, I knew everyone else in the country was doing exactly the same thing. Watching big Jean Beliveau, "Boom Boom" Geoffrion, the Pocket Rocket and Dickie Moore. I had their bubble-gum hockey cards. I'd study their pictures for hours, look at the way they held their sticks, how they taped their hockey socks, how they laced their skates—zigzag or straight across, the kind of stick they used, the curve it had. I was a Canadiens fan because they loved the game, loved it more than anyone else. They were just like me.

★　★　★

It was a harmless, nothing shot. Jim just tried to dump the puck into Rousseau's end, so he fired it hard at the corner. It flew up and caught the mesh right by one of the wooden posts and bounced out in front of the net. Roddy slapped it in, between the goalie's legs. Our fans had had little to cheer about, and so they cheered long and hard, even if not quite as long and hard as before. The red light was an ember of hope. But time was almost up. Five–fifteen left to play. Rousseau had outplayed us all period and most of the game. Tilt looked at us and nodded. "Okay guys, let's get something going." He pointed at me. "You stay. Cam, take right wing."

I looked. Shock, then anger welled up like a storm. Tilt motioned to me with a smile. "Wait. Just wait a sec," he said. "Quick changes now," he yelled to the guys on the ice.

Cam got the puck right from the face-off. He passed to
Bryan charging at the blue line. Murray followed close
behind. Bryan dropped it back, raced in. Murray shot. The
goalie stopped it with his blocker. Into the corner. Rousseau
tried to clear it. Trevor stopped it on the boards. He fired it
back into the corner. Four–fifteen on the clock. The crowd
sensed the time, too; they were coming alive, urging us,
looking for a miracle. The line came off. Our second line
raced into Rousseau's end; Mark poke-checked their
defenseman as he carried it out. Sent the puck spinning
toward the goal. It was batted away to the blue line, but
Peter stopped it with his skate, kept it in. He wound up. A
slap shot zinged past the bodies in front of the net like a bullet. CLANG! He hit the post. The crowd groaned. Two–fifty-
seven. The third line spilled over the boards. Desperation
drove us now. I looked at Tilt, cursed him. Mike slammed
the Rousseau left-winger into the boards. The puck slid
back to the line. Peter shot. The puck was two feet off the
ice. A hundred miles an hour. Roddy, standing in front of
the net, lifted his stick. He turned the blade just so, deflected the puck. The goalie went one way, the puck the other,
into the corner. Into the net. An explosion of noise that
would not stop. One–ten. Everyone on their feet now.
Every cowbell jangling. Every trumpet screeching. Tilt
looked at me, nodded. I was on.

★   ★   ★

We were milking. Dad had old Blue because she was
ornery. I had Daisy, a Holstein, because she wasn't. The cows
were side by side in the stall and we both sat on short old
stools, with our heads bent over against the cows. The barn
was quiet except for the rhythmic hiss as streams of milk cut
through rising foam in the pails. Blue had had a piss and the
hot sweet smell of it filled the air. She hadn't bothered to lift

her tail, all the better to swat Dad with. It's not as if there were flies. It was forty below.

Dad was the kind of guy who, when I got three goals and a penalty, would talk about the penalty. I had some bad news for him.

"Dad?" I said, finally getting up the nerve.

"Yeah?"

"I got in a fight last night." Waiting. "I got a game misconduct."

The milking stopped. Silence. Just the cows chewing hay. "Jesus H. Christ." Said in a soft low exhalation. This was not a good sign. The milking started, no soft hiss anymore, angry blasts of milk strafing the pail. Dad cleared his throat. I started milking, hanging onto Daisy's tits like a shipwrecked sailor.

"I'd sure like to know why you're screwing up your hockey like you do." I burrowed my head further into Daisy's warmth. "You know, buster, you can skate the pants off just about anyone. You can stickhandle. You can make plays. You got a helluva wrist shot. You beat a goalie in Riverside two weeks ago from outside the blue line! You know the game as well as anyone."

He was winding up now, picking up speed. "And what do you do? You just piss it away. You get rid of the puck like it's a hot potato. You don't take charge. You don't go into the corners and check like Bryan. You don't back-check like Roddy. You got all this talent and you just throw it away. And just to add icing on the bloody cake, you're sitting in the penalty box because you got a chip on your shoulder and you're goddamn fighting. You're sure not doing your team any good. And you're embarrassing yourself to boot. So just what the hell is the matter with you? That's what I'd like to know."

Milk ripped in torrents slashing through foam. Then

finally, the streams weakened, a few last squeezes. The wooden stool grated on the cement. Dad got up, came around, looked at me. The anger was going down. Bewilderment, frustration, but the white heat had passed. Just red now. A hint of relief. "Well?"

"I dunno." I blew out a long ribbon of fear.

"Well, nobody else has the answer. Nobody else is going to tell you why or what to do or how to do it, you know. Not Tilt, not me, not anybody. This is something you have to go inside for. You have to figure it out." Almost normal, almost caring now. "So think about it. Okay?" He turned and walked down the barn. The door rolled open and shut.

★ ★ ★

Forty-five seconds to go. End of the season, end of Midgets, end of everything. Something took hold of me, grabbed me, filled me up, shook me by the shoulders, something powerful from deep within that had been building since this morning's walk, maybe longer. I grabbed the puck in the corner, wheeled in a circle like on a frozen farmhouse puddle, got away from the snarling left-winger, stick flailing. A stride, a long powerful stride, a Maurice Richard stride cutting, pushing steel into the ice. Speed now, the Rocket going faster, Number 9 blasting, feeling the wind of my own making, deking around defensemen stuck in their surprise like green pins, wheeling by them, past the cattails, the snowy boards, past frozen boots, and George and Marg, and Mom and Dad, past the turkey, past everyone I ever knew, heading for the target, moving in the frozen dark, moving toward the circle of light at the end of the rink, the dark rink, where everything was shut out except that small rectangle of net with Jim and Barry, with Terry Sawchuck, with Gump Worsley, with Johnny Bower standing, waiting. Stick cradling the puck, one side then the other, body leaned over, legs driving, blades flashing like bayonets, breath like a locomotive, across the blue line, defenseman's stick rapping on my ass, the defenseman's stick ripping across my waist, an arm pulling. Twisting. Falling! *Shit, I'm falling!* My legs go out. *No! No!* Down we go, defenseman and me, sliding, sliding, the puck goes twirling, a black disk spinning on its edge through a blizzard of snow-covered ice, stick stretched out, arms stretched in front of me, head lifting off the ice, goalie going down in front of us, a green wall, sliding, I push my stick, flat along the ice, push it at the twirling puck, it flies up and out of sight, up and over the green pin of a goalie, somewhere, out of desperate reach, somehow, the puck goes rolling, rolling into the crocheted net.

Around us was a wall of sound, wrapping us in a wild, delirious cocoon. Screaming Tigers piled on like football players. A mound of bodies, punching, crazy, laughing, yelling. Tilt, hands and knees on the ice, peering through the muddle with teary eyes. Everywhere yelling, leather gloves pounding into leather, cowbells clanging, trumpets, whistles, farm women in their kerchiefs, weeping, tobacco scoreboard girl smiling, farmers' faces cracked with jagged nervous laughter, Danny Gallivan speechless. Five minutes, six, maybe ten. The puck is finally dropped. There are seconds left. A few swats at it. The horn goes. Tie game! Overtime! And still the noise, thundering from that ice-cold rink, thundering through the graceful, curving beams, through the roof and out into the dark cold prairie night.

★   ★   ★

A knock. *Who knocks at a dressing room door?* "Yeah? Come in."

The door opened a crack. Mom peeked in, Dad behind her. "Come in."

They walked in like guests at the wrong wedding. Mom

in her brown Army & Navy coat and blue wool hat, graying blonde hair showing at the sides. Dad wearing his city carcoat, green cap and permanent farmer tan. They sat down on the bench across the corner from me. No one spoke for a minute. I was dressed, had my feet up, legs crossed on my hockey bag, arms folded, slouched into my leather hockey jacket. There was a garbage can in the middle of the floor, wads of black tape around it, a pile of towels with Dennis's blood on them. Wet spots where snow had melted. The broken blade of a stick. In the corner, the rest of it, leaning.

Mom fiddled with her gloves. Dad cleared his throat. "Well, that sure was a great game."

I studied my boots, nodded slightly.

"You played so well," said Mom, her green eyes probing. "Tilt said he'd been waiting for that all season, that he knew you had it in you."

A smile.

"We all knew," Dad said. "How'd that puck go in on that goal, anyway?"

"I dunno," I laughed. "I haven't got a clue." More silence.

"That scout told Tilt you guys played with a lots of **guts.**" Dad, careful with his words like he was gathering **eggs.** "He's talking to a couple of guys from Rousseau." A pause. "No one from here."

"Yeah, he told me."

"There's no shame in losing, you know," said Mom. "You did everything you could. They were just a stronger team."

"People are saying it's the best game they've ever seen here," said Dad.

I uncrossed my arms, tucked my hands into my pockets. "I'm not upset, you know." I sat up a little, put my boots on the floor, stared at the bloody towels. "Actually, I'm pretty happy." I could feel Mom and Dad's eyes, waiting.

"I've . . . uhhh . . . I've always been so afraid."

"Afraid?" Dad asked. Mom put a hand on his knee.

A shrug. "I dunno, of being good maybe. Tonight . . . was incredible because the fear was . . . gone. I felt like . . . like I could do . . . anything."

I picked up some crinkled black tape, rolled it into a sticky ball. "Except, what if I walk out of here and go to some party and never get it back again?"

I tossed the ball at the garbage can. Missed.

"Well," said Dad slowly, "maybe that's not the end of it." He paused. "Maybe it's just the beginning." He stood up. Mom followed. "Guess that's up to you."

Mom stood square in front of me. "We're very proud of you."

Dad slapped my knees with his gloves. "Yup," he said. A crooked smile. They turned for the door. "See you tomorrow."

"Have fun," said Mom.

"'Night." I said. And then, "Thanks." A pause. "Thanks for everything."

But the door had swung shut. I sat there for a minute or two longer, then stood up, slung my hockey bag over my shoulder, grabbed my stick, looked around the room. Slowly I inhaled the smell of wet leather, of black tape and painted wood, the sweet smell of sweat. I went out. The lights on the ice had been turned off. The outside door closed behind me with a bang. The sound echoed through the empty rink.

Sun Dogs

WISPS OF SNOW swept across the flat white fields. They swooped down through the ditch, parted slightly for bristles of fireweed and thistle that the mowers had missed in the fall, then licked across the frozen gravel road with ragged tongues. Sometimes in bad weather, when the fields and road and sky are like one seamless white carpet, the weeds are the only way you can tell where the road ends and the ditch begins.

Mom was driving. We were coming home from church in Lashburg, my sisters Nicky and Tracey-Lynn in the back seat. It was March and we were itching for spring after months of short dark days and numbing cold. But spring was just a faint scent in the air on certain mornings, and this morning it wasn't there at all.

"Sun dogs," I said to Mom, who was pressed up against the wheel, straining to see the road. They were shimmering white spots hanging low in the sky on either side of the sun—light refracted by ice crystals. It meant the air higher up was cold. At ground level it was ten below, almost balmy by Saskatchewan standards.

"Weather's going to change," said Mom. She raised her eyes to look at the sky, then dropped them quickly back. "We could be in for a storm." An abandoned red brick church loomed out of the whiteness on our right. In summer, after suppers, I often rode my bike there, pried open the door with a screwdriver, and played "Bumble Boogie" on the old pump organ. Mom slowed to turn left. We were a mile from the farm.

"So what'd you think of Harry's sermon today?" The white Fairlane chugged around the corner. Mom pressed the gas, gripping the wheel tightly as she picked up speed. The girls were arguing over which Beatle was better looking.

"Don't know, haven't thought about it," I lied.

I'd been paying more attention to the fact that Anna-Maria was in the choir. I liked her, had actually sung some hymns out loud thinking it would score a few points. But then Harry'd started talking about sin, something I knew a little about. He had fixed me with a steely Christian gaze and asked in his thick Dutch accent, "Vat if every time we did sometink wrong, we pounded a nail into a door?" He paused to let us squirm a little, then drilled a look right through me. "And if every time we did sometink right, we pulled a nail out?" We were quiet as barn cats, waiting for the thundering fist of a punch line. "Yet even if we pulled out all de nails, we'd have still a door full of nail holes." There was much coughing and rustling after that, and later the collection plate was overflowing.

"I guess he was saying behave yourself if you want to keep your front door looking nice," I said. Mom laughed, her blonde hair poking out from under a burgundy paisley scarf. I figured mine probably looked more like a screen door.

Maybe it was the weather, maybe it was because it was Sunday, but when we got home I was restless. Dad was sitting at the kitchen table reading a *National Geographic*. The coal-wood stove was going. He didn't go to church much, said he worshiped at the church of the great outdoors.

Which was a good idea in summer. I went upstairs, put on jeans, thick wool socks, a heavy wool sweater. "I'm riding down to the river," I said as I strode into the kitchen, grabbed an apple and opened the fridge to get some cheddar cheese.

Mom looked up from cutting celery. Tuna sandwiches for lunch. "You think that's a good idea? You saw those sun dogs." *Why is it when parents ask a question, there's always an opinion behind it?*

"Hell. Radio didn't say anything about a storm. Might be three days before anything happens."

"Stop swearing in my kitchen." Worry flashed across her blue eyes like the aurora borealis, her knife poised in midair. "You know how unpredictable the weather is." She turned to Dad, up to his eyeballs in some Mayan dig. "Bart?"

Dad lowered his magazine. "He'll be fine." He looked at me. "Just hightail it home if you see anything coming, okay?"

Nicky flounced in. She was thirteen and looking for action. "Can I come, too?"

"No, stupid. You don't even know where I'm going."

"Don't call your sister stupid." Dad was glowering now.

"Right." I nodded, turned and headed for the door, reaching up on my way by the fridge to grab some matches from the old tin match dispenser. It was the smartest thing I did that day.

"Come on, Scamp," I said to our beagle. "Let's go." But he just lay there and wouldn't budge. *That's a new one,* I thought and walked out the door.

The sky was the color of bath water. The sun glowed dimly like a pale moon with two small discs on either side. I wondered, as I walked to the barn, how the ice crystals in sun dogs stayed up in the air when snowflakes and hail didn't.

Paddy was at the fence by the barn paddock, ears forward, head up and over the top rail like he knew something was up. I whistled. He whinnied back. Paddy was a Palomino quarter horse, a gelding. I'd bought him for $275 a couple of years ago, money I'd made from summer jobs, mowing ditches for the municipality, digging culverts into roads with a pick and shovel. He sure was a pretty horse. Not big, but he had a nice golden coat with white mane and tail and forelock, and a white blaze down his nose. Dad said Paddy didn't know he was a horse at all. Thought he was a human or maybe the world's biggest lapdog.

He snorted with that little tremolo through the nose that horses do, and I snorted right back in the way that people with horses do. I opened the fence, grabbed Paddy's halter and walked him out to the front door. I went into the barn and got the bridle and saddle and blanket. The blanket had been my grandfather's. The saddle I'd bought from an old cowboy out east of town. I was tightening the cinch when Paddy cranked his head around. His nose went right to my jacket pocket like a bee to a flower. He'd found the apple.

"Hey, you fat four-legged thief!" I laughed, offering him the McIntosh from Ontario. He took the whole thing in his mouth like a Lifesaver. Paddy looked a little ratty with his long winter coat, and his hooves needed clipping. I figured I'd curry him when we got back.

I swung up in the saddle and settled into the butt-worn seat, enjoying the creak of the leather, the warm smell of horse. We walked past the house and down the lane, then west between the fields toward the river, the South Saskatchewan River. There aren't many rivers in this province and I always felt lucky we had one just three miles from the farm. It was like a magnet for our family, summer and winter—a destination when there was nothing to do and nowhere to go. Every year we made bets on when the ice would go out. Sometimes we could hear the groaning of ice from the house and, once, the roar of it as a jam broke and swept downstream. I wanted to be there if it happened again. At least I wanted to see what condition the ice was in. I nudged Paddy in the sides with my work boots and he grudgingly started to trot.

We weren't exactly horse people. I was a little scared of Paddy, afraid of falling off and getting hurt. It had happened a couple of times at a dead gallop and I'd limped for weeks. Paddy wasn't broken in. He just tolerated us until he didn't want to anymore, then he'd head for the barn. We'd hired this cowboy once to come and break him for us, a little Japanese guy named Snowball. He was a cruel bastard. He raked Paddy's sides with his spurs, trying to get him to buck. After about five minutes Paddy's sides were covered with blood. Dad was so mad he was shaking. He told Snowball he'd shoot him if he didn't get off. I put ointment on the wounds, but the spur marks were still there. So we babied Paddy even more after that.

We followed a prairie trail down between two stubble fields. The straw from last year's crop stuck through the snow like an old bachelor's three-day beard. Straight ahead I could just make out the hills on the far side of the river, a dark bluish smudge below the thin gray line of horizon. "It's colder than I thought," I said to Paddy. I pushed my brown Stetson down further. "Wish I had my green toque." I slowed Paddy to a walk and did up the top button on my heavy denim jacket. I was glad for the fleece lining and my wool long johns.

"Damn!" I was looking down at the snow sifting through the stubble. The wind had changed. In just a few minutes it had swung around. Now it was blowing from the north. I turned in the saddle and looked back home. We were still about two miles from the river. "Better not be long," I said and gave Paddy a little kick in the ribs with my heels. I figured horses are like motorcycles. You have to kick 'em through the gears one at a time. Paddy broke into an amble but shook his head and sidestepped like he didn't want to go anywhere but back to the barn.

"Come on, you old plug, or I'll haul you to the glue factory." Paddy compromised with a trot while he was thinking it over, and when I kicked him again he consented to a canter.

Suddenly a white spot straight ahead of us exploded out of the snow and ran. Snowshoe! Paddy jumped, went straight-legged, came down hard on all fours. He twisted sideways to the left and launched himself into a gallop across the field. I grabbed the horn to hang on, dropped the left rein. Runaway! I leaned forward, reached down, tried to snag the rein as it lashed the air. Paddy stepped on it once, twice. It stretched, then snapped loose, whipped forward past his ear. The ground below raced by, a blur of seething, plunging white. My head was full of the sounds of leather, horse hooves beating the frozen ground beneath the crusty snow. Finally I grabbed the rein, leaned back and hauled in hard on both reins. Paddy slowed, then lurched to a stop and stood there, belly heaving under me, blowing steam out his nostrils. My heart was racing, blood pounded in my ears. "Paddy!" I yelled. "Haven't you seen a stupid rabbit before?"

With that out of his system, Paddy settled into an easy lope. In a few minutes, we were out of the fields and weaving through sage brush and buffaloberry trees. As we passed, the wind blew icy combs of hoarfrost off the branches. We headed west to a barbed-wire fence, then followed it until we reached the gate. It was open. There were no cattle out here in winter. We rode through. Soon we were in the hills—khaki green in summer, now white and round and smooth, gouged with ravines, where old creeks had carved their way down to the river. I angled south toward the Seaton ravine, just a dip in the land full of chokecherry bushes. As the ravine deepened, the bushes became gnarly gray sticks of maple, then poplar and finally willows by the water. We walked along the ridge, and from on top of Paddy I could see the river. The ice was cracked like a hard-boiled egg. Pressure ridges crisscrossed from one side to the other half a mile away. It looked ominous—like a rattler ready to strike.

We followed the ravine and where it widened finally, we angled down a big hill to the bottom, where Paddy waded through chest-high drifts to reach the shore. Cakes of dirty ice full of wind-blown sand had pushed up on the frozen banks, had bulldozed young willows and driftwood into piles. We stopped. Paddy sniffed at some ragged cattails while I sat there taking in the scene. I thought of the early explorers seeing this for the first time, cataloguing each geographic feature, each sensation and thought for their journals and maps. Did they think it was an empty, lonely and bleak land? Or did they think, like the Indians, that it was beautiful? The Plains Cree had been here for ten thousand years. It was their garden, a gift from the Creator. I imagined a hunting party and I was one of them. On pinto ponies, with strings of dead snowshoes and white-tailed deer dangling head down across the horses, we returned to our tepees hidden from the wind in the deepest coulees, where sweet plumes of woodsmoke rose in the air.

Paddy snorted. I snapped back to reality. Out on the river white waves of snow were drifting across the ice, curling over the ridges. The wind had picked up! The far shore had disappeared. I looked up. A mass of low clouds, dark with snow, was barreling along the river toward us. My heart jerked into high speed, a surge went right to my legs and hands. *Storm!* I'd stayed too long! I looked up at the sun dogs. "Dammit, I'm stupid."

Dad's words poked at me. "He'll be fine. Just hightail it home if you see anything coming, okay?"

"Come on," I yelled to Paddy. The tension in my voice surprised me. "Let's get out of here." I pulled hard on the right rein. Paddy wheeled around and I kicked, nosed him toward the snowdrift we'd broken through just minutes before. Paddy wanted to follow our tracks along the side of the ravine where we'd come down. But I was in a hurry now. I wanted to get to the top of the hill and run like hell for home. I kicked Paddy again and yanked left on the rein. "We're going straight up, big guy. Let's go."

Horses, like dogs or any animal, can smell fear. And they sure know when a storm's brewing. Paddy charged the hill. I leaned down close to his neck with the reins held tight. We were halfway up when it happened.

Crack!

There are certain sounds I'll never forget as long as I live: the thwack of a baseball into my glove, the puck on my stick in an empty rink, Paddy's leg snapping. A small wet sound, like a carrot breaking.

Before I knew what it meant, Paddy was falling forward and sideways to the right. And I was flying over his right shoulder, watching in slow motion—his mane, his shoulder rolling, the saddle falling away under me. I landed in a fury of writhing snow and mane and leather reins. Paddy screamed, a horrible high-pitched sound I'd never heard before. I scrambled to my knees. He was laying with his back to me, thrashing, his legs flailing the air. His right front leg had snapped, above his hoof, just above the fetlock. It was swinging back and forth like a cloth on the wind each time he kicked. I threw myself onto Paddy's neck, spread my arms over him. "Paddy, Paddy! Don't!" I yelled.

But his mouth was twisted, his eyes bulged wild with pain. Paddy jerked his head, rolled, struggled to get up. He lost his balance, put his weight on his broken foreleg. It bent over at right angles in the snow. Paddy screamed again, but stood and hopped wildly up the hill on three legs, fell again, rolled, hooves stabbing the air, chunks of snow flying. The saddle slipped down his side, stirrups kicked out, reins whipping the air around his head. I scrambled after him, yelling, falling in the snow. Paddy turned and lunged back down the hill. Half hopping, half slipping, his nostrils flared, his eyes huge. He came right at me. "Paddy!" I jumped and rolled out of the way. Paddy brushed by, the saddle hanging under him now, stirrups banging his feet, kicking up snow. Paddy lurched toward the willows, down where the snow was deep in the brush in the bottom of the ravine. He ploughed in, falling on his side, thrashing. Again he struggled to get up. A few more lunges. Then finally he stopped, up to his chest in the soft deep drift.

I ran and slid down after him. "Paddy, Paddy." I was crying. Paddy's head was bowed, his sides heaving. I walked up slowly, waded up to my waist in the snow. I put a hand on his rear. He was sweating, in shock, in danger now of getting a chill that could kill him. *Kill him! He's broken his damn leg!* My mind was going a hundred miles an hour but I couldn't think. I just needed to get up by Paddy's head, grab the reins, calm him down, stop him from hurting himself anymore.

I worked through the snow beside him, keeping my hands on Paddy's flank, talking to him in a low voice. "Paddy . . . take it easy, big guy."

Slowly I ran my hand along his neck, touched the side of his face. "Atta boy, take it easy. It's okay." I saw why his head was bowed. The reins were caught on something in the snow. I bent down, pushed the snow away with my gloves. And then I saw his leg.

"Ugh." The sight of it sucked the air right out of me. The leg was folded forward at an awful angle. The jagged broken bone had punched through the skin, had poked bright red holes in the snow. I could see white tendons glistening. *Why isn't it gushing blood?*

"Careful, big guy, don't worry. I won't hurt you." I brushed the snow away and found the rein snagged on a branch. Slowly I pulled it out of the snow, talking all the while. "When we're outta here, I'm going to fix your leg and give you the best meal you've ever had in your life, Paddy boy. Chopped oats and mash with apples, lots of nice fresh hay. You like that, big guy?" I stood up slowly, let the reins fall. Paddy was still breathing in short jagged gasps. I kept one hand on his flank and moved back to undo the cinch.

"Gotta get this saddle off. Then you'll feel better, won't you?" The saddle was jammed in the snow under Paddy so the D-ring of the cinch was now up on his back. I undid it and carefully pulled the saddle out from under him, then tossed it and the blanket into the snow.

I stood there for a minute to catch my breath, to think. The awfulness started to sink in. *We're in big trouble.* I checked my watch for the first time that day: 3:30. It'd be dark in less than an hour. I couldn't leave Paddy and go for help. We were three miles from home and there was a blizzard coming, maybe minutes away. Anyway, I wasn't dressed for walking home, and only dead men go walking in a prairie blizzard. If there was a whiteout I could stumble around in circles until I froze to death. The wind had picked up. And snow was falling. It was too late. I was frozen with fear.

I imagined Mom and Dad at the kitchen window, maybe the upstairs bedroom, faces full of worry. "Maybe Dad will come in the tractor," I said out loud. But that wouldn't do Paddy any good unless he brought the stoneboat. And there'd be no reason for him to think of that. I knew what I had to do. I just didn't know how.

"Gotta get you out of this deep snow, boy."

A gust of wind swooped down the hill, lashed us with snow, dumped snow down my neck. *My hat!* Panic welled up inside me again. I guessed I'd lost it when Paddy went down. Somewhere on the hill. I was sweating, too. *I could die out here if I don't find it.* It seemed like such a trivial thing, but in winter small mistakes can kill you. "Be right back, Paddy."

I shivered as I climbed up the hill through the mess Paddy and I'd made in the snow. I stopped where I thought we'd been when it happened, kicked the snow around with my boots and found something else I was looking for. I dropped to my knees and swept away the snow with my hands. A badger hole, much bigger than a gopher hole, with a frozen pile of dirt at his doorstep. It had been hidden under the snow. An ugly black hole in the white. *Maybe this will kill my horse.* Maybe—and I could hardly even think this thought—*maybe it'll kill me.* I stood, eyes squinting, tears streaming down my face. I looked up at the sky and yelled, "GODDAMN YOU ALL TO HELL!"

I'd never felt so empty and alone and afraid in my life. I dropped to my knees and buried my face in my leather gloves. Shame splattered me like battery acid. *This wasn't His fault, you idiot. This was YOUR idea in the first place. YOU stayed too long. YOU chose to charge up that hill like some TV cowboy.*

There was no time for that. I got up, spotted my hat at the bottom of the hill by some bushes. I scrambled down, shook the snow out and put it on. The band was cold and wet. I was shivering. Fear, like ice-cold water in a metal tank, rose inside me.

Can't let that happen. Gotta stay calm. We gotta get out of this.

Paddy hadn't moved. His slumping back was covered with a thin layer of snow like icing sugar. I brushed it off, put my hand on him. He was shivering, too. I waded up to his head in the trampled drift. "Gotta make a path for you boy. Gotta get you into these trees, into some shelter." Even the word *shelter* seemed too much to hope for. It was getting dark quickly now, and at night there would be no shelter anywhere from the cold. The sky was gray-black. Snow swirled overhead and sifted down the messed-up hill. Our tracks, all signs of Paddy's accident, would soon be gone. A magpie shrieked in the wind. I looked around, saw nothing but the twisted tines of trees reaching up to the passing sky.

I began to clear a path in front of Paddy. I pushed through the snow with my legs together, beating the snow down with my boots. I pushed snow to the sides with my arms and gloves. We only had about fifteen feet to go. But the question was: would Paddy move? Would he hop on one front leg? Or would he freak out again and hurt himself more?

Paddy looked like a broken old toy, his body sagging. He barely raised his head as I approached. "Hey, big guy. Got to move you, just a bit. Then you can rest."

He leaned his head against me as I talked, as I stroked the velvety side of his nose. "I know you don't want to move but we have to. I'm so sorry." My eyes were about three inches from his big brown eye. *Come on, buddy,* I said with my eyes to his. And then, as if in answer, Paddy raised his head and snorted.

I grabbed the reins. "Okay, Paddy, come with me. Come." I pulled on the reins slowly. They went taut. Paddy did nothing but look at me with his sad eyes, bottomless, full of pain.

"Come on, big guy. It's your only chance."

And then something seemed to happen inside of him. I

can't say what it was. It was almost like he roused himself, got bigger. Paddy started to move. Slowly he raised his right leg, the broken foot dangling. And then he hopped on his left leg. Three hop-steps, then he stopped. The right hoof hovered above the snow. Paddy was breathing hard again. The vibrations must have hurt like crazy.

"I'm so sorry I got you into this, Paddy. Good boy. Just a few more like that." I gave the reins another tug. Again I sensed a rising in him. He neighed, not a shrieking neigh like before, but still there was pain in it. He took another hop-step and then another, and in a minute we were in the trees at the bottom of the ravine.

"Atta boy. What a great horse you are, Paddy boy. Okay, this is where we're spending the night. I'm going to build you a shelter right here, but you've got to lay down right now."

I was running out of time. It was almost dark. I needed to find wood and brush, to put up something to keep the snow and wind off us. All the time, just under the surface, fear was rippling, cold water in a black tank, fear that none of this was going to do any good, that I was going to lose my horse.

"Now, Paddy, lay down." I pulled the reins. "Right here, Paddy boy. I'm sorry, this is going to hurt again. Come on, lay down." For a horse that wasn't trained, he seemed to know what I wanted. Maybe he sensed that this was his only chance. Slowly Paddy folded his hind legs under him and sat down in the snow. Then he dropped his front quarters down, neighed again at the pain of it and flopped over onto his side, breathing hard.

I dropped to my knees by his side, brushed snow away from his head. I stroked his cheeks, patted his neck. "You are the bravest horse in the world." Paddy just lay there looking at me. Gently I took his bridle off.

Then I went to work. I stood, wiped the snow off my

jeans, frozen stiff from the knee down. I fished my jackknife out of my pocket, the bone-handled knife Grandma had given me for my birthday last year. My fingers were freezing. I fumbled with the big blade, finally got it open and cut the reins from the rings attached to the bit. I found a small tree growing, an inch thick, bent it over, broke it off. Then broke it again into five lengths a foot and a half long. I knelt by Paddy's broken leg.

"This is going to hurt again, Paddy boy. But I've got no choice." I brushed the snow away from his leg, saw the white jagged cannon bone jutting out of the torn skin. I pushed my hands under his leg in the snow. "Sorry." With my right arm wrapped around it, I pulled on Paddy's hoof. He snorted, that was all. The bone disappeared back inside the skin. I pulled again, then pushed at the crack with my left hand, pushing the bones together.

"I sure hope that's better, big guy. 'Cause I don't know what the hell I'm doing." Gently I placed the sticks around his leg, then wrapped the rein around and around them, slipping the ends under themselves to hold it tight. "It's not too pretty but it might work." *And this from a guy who can't stand the sight of blood!*

"Okay, gotta get moving."

I saw a couple of small trees, dead and leaning over. They were about three inches thick. I snapped them off from their frozen, rotten roots, then dragged them over to Paddy. I held one end up and put my boot on the tree, broke it into pieces four feet long. I put three of them by Paddy's head, grabbed one half of the remaining rein, lashed the poles together at the top so they formed a tepee. Paddy lay still, watching with one wary eye. "Atta boy. You rest. I'll have this up in a minute."

I took three more short poles and made another tepee near Paddy's rump. I got a ten-foot pole and lay it across the two tepees, so it ran above Paddy about three feet high. I needed a bunch of short poles now, branches, bushes, anything to lean against the long pole and make a roof over Paddy and me.

But I had run out of time.

The storm descended like a hammer, driving away the last shred of daylight. Wind whistled through the treetops above us, pellets of wet snow stinging like tiny bullets. Paddy raised his head and whinnied. "Down boy. It's okay." But it wasn't. The saddle! I'd left it out in the drift. I ran to get it, stumbling and tripping through the brush in the dark. The saddle was already covered with six inches of snow. I felt around for the blanket. Got it! I lugged them back through the bush to our campsite. "Campsite!" I said out loud.

I pulled the saddle alongside Paddy's head, propped it up in the snow with the leather seat facing into the wind, the sheepskin on the underside next to Paddy's head. Maybe it would keep some of the wind out of his face. I grabbed the horse blanket. "Okay, big guy." I unfolded it, lay it across Paddy's wet neck, across his legs and withers. Paddy opened his eyes.

"That's for you, buddy."

I had to finish the shelter. There was no choice. My leather gloves were wet, my fingers were stiff with cold, my toes were tingling. I'd have to stop soon and bang them to keep them from freezing, just like when we played hockey at Uncle George's slough and it was thirty below. Snow blew down my neck. *Why didn't I bring a scarf?* Mom would have the last laugh at that one. All my life she'd been telling me to wear my toque and scarf. And all my life I'd laughed and walked out the door.

I felt my way around in the dark like a blind man, rummaging through the bush, breaking off branches, crawling back with them, leaning them against the pole above Paddy.

It was slow work and it wasn't doing a thing to keep snow out. Every few trips, I'd check on Paddy, say hello, wipe the snow off. Sometimes Paddy shuddered. But he didn't move and he didn't make a sound.

When I had enough branches on the roof, I scrambled back to the brush at the edge of the trees. I dropped to my knees and tore at the bushes. Hunched over in the driving snow, I half hauled, half dragged armloads of them back. I laid them sideways to the other poles, pushed them tightly together, trying to thatch a roof. I was dog-tired but I couldn't think about that. I had to get the shelter built. Or Paddy and I might never see daylight again.

It was hard to keep track of direction in the dark. Once I thought I was lost and an electric shock of fear went through me. I stopped. *Don't panic. Don't move until you figure out where you are.* I looked for a minute, eyes straining against the snow, the dark. And there among the dark shapes of the trees, I saw the darker roofline of our shelter. *Better not let that happen again.*

Once I'd covered the back of the lean-to with brush, I started on the two sides. I was exhausted now, running on fear. When I couldn't pull or break any more bushes, I went behind the shelter and started scooping wet snow onto the roof with my gloves, then my hat. I was lucky—if you could call it that. It was a March blizzard and the temperature wasn't as cold as in January or February. I packed the wet snow and kept shoveling until I had created a solid wall on three sides of Paddy.

I crawled around to the front of the shelter, shaking like a loader motor. "All right, Paddy. I'm here now." Paddy didn't move. I couldn't see his face in the dark. I crawled between his front and back legs, up to his belly, swept the snow off him and patted him. "So what do you think, big guy? Think it'll keep us going till morning?" Still no sound,

68

no movement. I sat down in the snow and leaned against
Paddy's belly, careful not to touch his leg.

I was finished. I'd done all I could do, but I'd paid a ter-
rible price. My hair was soaked with snow and sweat. I'd lost
a lot of body heat. I was shaking; my teeth were chattering.
I pushed my cold wet hat down, reached inside my jacket
and pulled up the collar of my sweater. I tugged at my jacket collar and scrunched up my shoulders as far as I could. I
had to do something about my toes. I made fists and pounded my knees, driving vibrations down into my boots to
increase circulation. It helped my fingers, too. After a few
minutes I could feel them again, a throbbing pain. I had my
back to Paddy, was leaning against his belly like a sponge
trying to soak up warmth, even give him some of mine.
"Maybe we'll save each other, Paddy old boy."

In the dark, snow flitted around us like blackflies. Drifts
piled up. I could feel them on Paddy's hind legs. The sound
was a roaring hiss, like a whisper turned up full blast.
Branches creaked, pellets of snow blasted the trees above.
"Jeez, Paddy, I wish you'd turn up the heat."

And then a beautiful thought popped to the surface like
a loon: "I've got matches!" They were in my shirt pocket. I'd
planned to smoke a cigarillo, which I'd forgotten. "We'll be
all right!" But a blast of wind snuffed out hope before it
could ignite. *I'll never be able to light a fire in this blizzard.
Maybe, if the wind dies down, if we live that long.* My spirits sank
as I slid down inside myself, searching for warmth, solace,
something.

In the black and awful dark, the answer slowly revealed
itself. I thought about Harry's sermon—was it only this
morning? I wondered what time it was. I couldn't see my
watch in the dark. I wondered how much time I had, we
had. I felt Paddy's chest, could feel the warmth, the faint
thump of his heart. I thought of nails in the door of my

soul. I thought of the stories I'd grown up with: dead hunters too drunk to get their car unstuck down by the river, found frozen the next morning in the shop of an abandoned farm, tar paper wrapped around their legs, piles of wooden matches at their feet. Their hands had been too cold to light them. Or the farmer, lost in the whiteout between his house and the barn, found by his wife the next morning, a frozen sculpture hanging on a barbed-wire fence. He'd missed his barn by twenty feet. *Am I about to pay for my sins? All those nails in the door? Will they find me curled up and frozen to my dead horse? Will the coyotes find us first?*

I started to count nails. I'd been rude again to Nicky this morning. When was the last time I'd been nice to her? I guess it was when she was three. I put the head back on her doll and gave her a kiss on the forehead and for some reason said, "Don't tell Mom." Since then, I'd made her life miserable. Pushed her down a hill and through a fence on her tricycle. It had taken twenty-three stitches to close up her leg. It was always something like that: a live mouse down her back, a dead chicken thrown into the girls' playhouse. Big brother stuff. Still, sitting there, I felt sick about it.

Tracey-Lynn was still too young to have gotten the full treatment. But I had called her ugly lots because she wore glasses. And I called her stupid when she practiced the piano. Mom was furious because Tracey-Lynn was just starting out. Otherwise I ignored her. Come to think of it, I didn't know my younger sister at all.

Mom! She'd be sick by now. I could just see her crying her eyes out, with all the lights on in case I was walking home in the blizzard. They'd be on the phone to all the neighbors, trying to figure out if we'd made it somewhere and what to do because we hadn't. They couldn't go out until the storm ended. It made me crazy. *It must be hell for them*. I thought of all the times I made her worry. Like when I hid in the doghouse when we had a house full of company for Sunday dinner. I didn't come when I was called. They searched the farm and even the dugout. Women were crying and men were grim—until they heard me sneeze. I got a licking that night and no food.

I thought of Mom and her garden, how hard she worked to weed and water it. And how much I hated it, how much I complained about weeding. "I notice you never complain when you're eating," she said one day in a fury. She was the one who said I could get straight A's if I wanted. I was always surprised how disappointed she was when I brought home mainly C's and B's. I knew I could do better, but Dad was right. I was lazy.

"You were a harder worker when you were ten than you are now," Dad had said not long ago. We'd been hauling wheat, shoveling in the bin, buried up to our asses, working around those rods that hold the granaries together. I'd been out with the boys the night before, sampling lemon gin and cheap cherry brandy.

I wasn't raised to be a farmer, but I was expected to do my share of the work. And yet, all I could think about was baseball or hockey or football, whatever sport happened to be in season, and when I wasn't playing or practicing, or fooling around with my cousins, or chasing girls, I was in my room or in the bunkhouse with my nose buried in a book. The thought struck me that I wasn't much of a son. And in a horrible moment, I wondered if Dad was lonely for me. "Ohhhh," I moaned, deeply ashamed.

Paddy answered with a snort. He stirred. I could sense him half raise his head. I rolled over, shocked to discover how stiff I was, locked into a crouch beside him. "It's okay, Paddy. You all right? That's a good horse." And then, "I love you, Paddy." Again my mind filled with regret. I thought of how little I rode this horse, this guy I'd worked so hard to get, had begged for, for so long.

"You've got to take care of him," they'd said.

"I will, I will," I'd promised. And I thought of how ragged he looked. Hadn't been brushed in days, maybe weeks. His hooves needed trimming, needed a farrier to get them back into shape. "I don't deserve you, Paddy. You're so incredible, I don't deserve you." I leaned into Paddy's side, my face up against his wet shivering belly.

"When we get out of here, I'm going to spoil you rotten, big guy." I stroked him, brushing off more snow. For some reason I thought of my teachers and the fat old geometry teacher I tormented.

"She's just trying to teach me something that might be useful some day, and all I do is make life so miserable for her she probably can't wait to get home." I was talking out loud now, getting sadder by the minute, horrified at my life as a big dumb jerk. And now I was going to die, maybe, in a goddamn snowdrift.

The icy, creeping regret, the fear, the cold—it all made me sleepy. The howling wind was like a numbing lullaby, the snow a soft deadly quilt. *Well, maybe people who die in storms get this way. They just slip away in a dream.*

I can't fall asleep!

I jumped up, or at least tried to. I crouched in front of the lean-to, tried to straighten. I was so stiff and cold. My toes were numb now, my fingers, too. "I'm freezing to death!" My words seemed mumbled and very small. I had to do something. *Is Paddy dying slowly in the dark, too?*

He could die right here and I won't even know it! I knelt down again and crawled to Paddy's head.

"Paddy, Paddy. You okay?" I felt his face, brushed a pile of snow away from his ears. No answer. I bent down low, put my ear to his nose. He was breathing!

"Don't die on me, Paddy. Please don't die. I'm so sorry I got you into this mess. I'm so sorry." Paddy answered with a small short sniff. It was a sweet sound.

"Okay, guy. Great. Now I gotta look after myself for a bit."

I got up. I started jumping up and down, spreading my legs one time, bringing them together the next, each time swinging my arms out to the side. What was this exercise called? *My mind. I can't think. I can't remember.*

And then I laughed out loud. I thought of my Uncle Norman. He would have had some wry comment that'd have me keeled over, laughing my guts out. Tears filled my eyes and I started jumping faster. I could feel my toes again. My fingers were hurting, which was a good sign. I wondered what time it was. *How long until morning? What if it's a three-day blizzard?*

Maybe it's what happens to people caught in disasters. They start making tough decisions, but by then the decisions aren't so tough. The idea just came. Maybe it had been there, lingering in the dark for a while. But I knew what I had to do, knew what would increase my odds of seeing daylight.

"I'm so sorry, big guy. I have to do this." I sat down on the snow between Paddy's front and hind legs, pulled his saddle blanket over my shoulders, left some to cover his legs, his withers. I worked my boots between Paddy's hind legs, where his balls would have been. He didn't move. I curled up, leaned sideways against his belly. My arms were folded against my chest, hands holding the blanket up close to my neck. That was awkward. I pulled them out, pressed them up against Paddy's belly. Better. My left side was almost warm. But the right side of me was freezing.

I can turn around later. I guess that's when I fell asleep.

Fitful images flew at me. People leering. A hockey coach

yelling, "Back-check!" Mom peering down. "You should have got straight A's." Harry standing in the pulpit with wild hair and a gigantic hammer, spitting nails from his mouth. A Christmas tree. All my family. Colored bubbles of laughter rising inside the lights. Grandma saying, "I wish you'd taken time to see me more." Dad with his shovel, frowning, up to his neck in wheat, drowning, yelling, "Shovel harder!" The farrier with his leather apron, his pick in Paddy's hoof, snarling at me, shaking his head. The vet, all dressed in white, with a huge needle spurting death, plunging it into Paddy's neck. The stuff spraying out Paddy's nose, his crying eyes. Splashing in my mouth, tasting like vinegar. I went down, down into soft clouds, drifting through whiteness. I was snow falling, falling in silence, into nothing.

I woke with a jerk. "Huh!" Panic. *How long? Am I frozen? My feet? Are they okay? My hands?* And then, relief. I was. *Did I just drift off? It feels like longer. Those awful dreams!* I sat up. Something was different. I looked around. Still pitch black. *Paddy! Is he dead?* I tore off my glove and put my hand against his side. He felt warm. He was breathing. And then I heard it—Silence! No wind howling. No hissing snow. The storm had passed. Hope surged inside me. "I can make a fire now, Paddy boy! We've got a chance." And then, "Hang in there, buddy. Hang in there."

This was going to be tricky. I had used every scrap of dead wood I could find to build the shelter. It was too dark to go very far. All I could do was feel around in the snow and find wood I'd missed. I started out on my hands and knees, dug down in the snow in front of our shelter. This would be the fire pit. Every twig, every little branch I put to the side in a pile. The ground at the bottom of the hole was covered with frozen leaves. They'd be wet. I'd have to put down a layer of wood and build the fire on that. *How many matches do I have?* Not many. Just a careless handful.

I crawled around in the snow, finding nothing at first. Then, bingo! A big branch under a foot of snow. I pulled at it. Judging from the weight, a long one. I pulled it up through the snow, followed it along by feel, hand over hand, snapping off branches as I went, holding onto them, afraid to drop them in case I might not find them again. It was good to do something, to feel hope again.

There were lots of twigs. I dragged the branch back to the shelter, pulled the thick end away and put the smaller branches near the fire pit so I could break them off and set the fire. My hands were still stiff with cold. My gloves were almost useless. If it hadn't been for the wool lining, I'd be a goner. Still I had to have everything ready before I risked taking them off and fumbling with the matches.

I thought of a Jack London story. A prospector had been caught in sixty-five below weather; his foot had gotten soaked in a creek. It was so cold he couldn't handle the matches. And when he finally got a fire going, snow fell off an evergreen and doused it. His dog sat and watched while he froze to death. I took my gloves off carefully.

I laid a row of small sticks across the bottom of the fire pit on the ground. Then a pile of twigs on top of that. There was grass in the snow. I pulled that, too, and rolled the blades of grass around my fingers into balls. Carefully I built a tepee of tiny sticks over the grass, then put bigger and bigger sticks on top. The larger ones I set to the side. I got my jackknife out and grabbed a bigger branch. Feeling my way in the dark, I carefully peeled the bark off, then dug in with the blade, carved a sliver of wood so it curled up. Slowly I moved the knife a little, dug the blade in and made another sliver. I did this over and over, sometimes slipping in the dark, trying not to cut myself, stopping to warm my fingers. In a few minutes I'd made a piece of tinder just the way Dad had showed me. But we'd never done it in pitch black before. And not in winter. I laid the stick down on the twigs so the flames from the grass would catch the shavings.

My fingers were numb. I tucked them into my pockets to warm them up before I tried the matches. I realized suddenly how precious these matches were. One little stick with chemicals on the end could mean my life and Paddy's. I fished them out of my shirt pocket and counted them. *Seven. Lucky number.* Hunched over the fire pit, I waited until my fingers were ready. Something made me look up. The trailing end of the storm system was passing by. Through the dark trees, between the clouds, I could see stars. And to the west, on the edge of the clouds, a silver rim of moonlight.

I struck the match on the zipper of my jeans. It flared up with a tiny flash, the light surprising after working blind for so long. Quickly I cupped my hands around it, moved it down into my fire pit and touched it to the grass. There was a brief hiss, a puff of smoke, and the match went out. *One down, six to go.*

And that's when a coyote yelped. Another one answered. And not far away. I stopped, held my breath for a second, reminding myself that coyotes aren't wolves. They're scared of people, too. *But how hungry are they? Another good reason to get this fire going.*

"Damn!" I dropped the second match in the snow. I'd held it too close, burned my fingers. I was nervous now. The third just flared and went out. The tether on my lifeline was getting shorter. I felt in the dark and opened the sticks in the pile a little to allow more air in. I moved the tinder stick down closer to the grass. The fourth. My hand shook. I struck the match and quickly angled the head down so the flame would burn upward on the stick, anything to give it a better chance. I moved it down to the tinder. A wisp of smoke, a curl of wood glowed red and then another. Suddenly a little flame licked up no bigger than a candle. I held my breath. Slowly, like a surgeon, I eased some grass and a twig toward the flame. They caught.

In a minute I had a small fire. There was no time for relief. I felt for the sticks I'd set aside, grabbed them, banged the snow off, then carefully placed each one, blowing gently on the flames, nursing them along. The wood was wet. Tiny wisps of steam rose up. I started stripping off the bark. Quickly I cut into the sticks with my knife, opening them up to expose the dry wood inside. It took five minutes, maybe more, of coaxing. Finally I had a fire. I reached for more wood. Bigger pieces. And then the first "snap" told me the fire was real. I piled everything I'd found onto that fire. I built a log house around the flames so as they rose, they dried the wood, warmed it, then ignited it. Sparks rose into the black and with them, my hopes. I held my fingers right in the flames. They were so cold I couldn't feel any pain. I rubbed them. Only then did I allow myself a brief sigh of relief. *Maybe we'll live after all.*

But I needed more wood. The flames were a foot high now, and for the first time since dusk I could see trees around us. And the drifts of snow that the blizzard had built. *My God! We're surrounded!* The lean-to was buried in snow, more like a cave with snow blown and curled in drifts around the sides enclosing us. I could see Paddy dimly, a white shape in the shadows. Not moving.

"Paddy? Paddy, boy? Are you still with me, big guy?" My breathing stopped again as I bent over him. Waiting.

His head stirred, his eye opened. "Oh God, Paddy. Thank you. Thank you for not being dead."

I rolled out of the way so he could see. "Look, we've got a fire, bud. This'll keep us going till morning. Till they come."

I stood up. The fire made wild dancing shapes on the closest trees but hardly a dent in the dark wall behind them.

I walked up to a small birch I hadn't seen before and pushed it. It didn't give. I tried another tree, a thin maple. It creaked. I grabbed it, rocked hard and snapped it off near the base. We were in luck. It was maybe twenty feet tall, the top out of sight in the dark. I pulled it beside the fire. I braced one end between two trees and stomped on it. It wouldn't break. I pulled it right over the fire so it would burn the tree in half. I'd feed the two ends into the fire later. A lazy man's fire.

The fire was going well now. But my hands and feet were still freezing, and clearing skies meant the temperature would drop. I stopped, crouched close as I could to the fire to warm my feet. I held my soaking gloves right in the flames. Steam swirled off them. The heat felt so good on my face. My eyes glazed over for a second as I stared at nothing. And then—*Where are those sparks? In the trees, just beyond the light. Did I see something? Coyote eyes? Shit. Couldn't be. Don't they know we're not good eating?*

Maybe it was just sparks; maybe I was too tired. The flames licked up into the darkness, two feet high, cracking, the wet wood hissing. *My watch! I'd forgotten. Five-thirty! Could it really be? Still two cold hours till light. Not enough wood. Maybe we won't make it. So sorry, everybody. So sorry for everything. Maybe no chance to be better.* My eyes were heavy. They wanted to close. I pitched forward, jammed my hands into the snow to keep from falling into the fire. *Got to have a nap.* I crawled back away from the pit, back into the shelter, tucked my boots between Paddy's legs again and huddled against my half-dead horse. "Just a little rest. I'll get more wood in a minute, Paddy boy. Don't die on me now. Please don't die."

Out of the corner of my eye, the last thing I saw, in the black wall beyond the trees, were twin sets of yellow glowing, reflected firelight dancing in the dark.

★　★　★

A buzz, low like a mosquito on a hot summer night. It
wouldn't go away. It got louder and louder. And then, a roar.
My eyes opened. Blinding white light. Blue. The roar still
there. Then a flash of red above the trees. A huge wide wing
of red! *Gunnar!*

His plane filled the ravine with sound. Searching for
me. It disappeared over the hill, the sound with it. I was
alive. "Gunnar!" I tried to yell but all that came out was a
ragged croak. I tried to get up, but I was stiff and cold to
the bone, my pants frozen solid. Paddy was covered with
snow. *Dead?* The whole world white, with shadows, a thin
wisp of smoke from my fire almost out, smoke still curling
up, as if from a cigarette, to the blue above. My heart was
pounding.

"Paddy. Paddy. They found us." I rolled away from
Paddy, staggered to my feet, almost falling into the fire. I
staggered like a drunk toward the path I'd made last night.
But there was no path. It was gone. Instead, a wall of white
ten feet high. I turned and ran, stumbling to the other side,
the leeward side of the ravine, ploughed through the trees,
then the brush, out into the full sunlight. The sound again.
The plane was coming back. I launched myself at the six-
foot snowbank, half crawling, half swimming across the top.
I was yelling. I don't know what.

The plane was lower this time, a hundred feet up
maybe, carving a red circle in the blue sky. I could see Gunnar at the window. I stood at the bottom of the hill, yelling,
waving both hands above my head. Gunnar waved, dipped
his wing and disappeared again. *He sees me.* On my hands
and knees, I scrambled up the side of ravine to the top. Gunnar turned, was coming back, the red wings tilting graceful-
ly, silver skis glistening in the sun. He was lower now, maybe

fifty feet, buzzing me. I was waving, crying, shrieking. The roar drowned out the sound. I saw him open the window and throw something out. A string of white unraveled like the tail of a kite and streamed down in a long, thin, white line—toilet paper!

I started laughing. Gunnar and Maggie were Dad and Mom's best friends. They lived just a couple of miles away. Gunnar often dropped a roll when flying over our farm. We'd run out and get it because there was always a note on the end that said "Coffee's on" or "Let's go golfing." Slowly the ribbon unfurled toward me. I ran to get it as Gunnar turned to make another pass. The streamer crumpled into the snow. I picked it up, hauled it in like fish line, looking for the end. And the note. In a hasty scrawl, he'd written, "Thank God you're alive."

There was another sound. I looked up. A tractor, a green John Deere, was coming along the crest of the hill toward me. They must have seen Gunnar turning, seen the toilet paper. And on the other side of the ravine, two yellow Ski-doos appeared. I waved again. The tractor was just like ours. I couldn't tell who was in the cab. I stood there waving. And then—as it came closer—I could see. It was Dad! And Mom was there, too, perched beside him. The big diesel engine belched smoke as Dad hit the throttle. The big black tires spun as they came toward me. They stopped. My uncles, George and Norm, roared up right behind them on their snowmobiles.

Dad opened the door of the cab. He was smiling, his bottom lip quivering. Mom was bawling her head off. The heat from the engine, from the cab, hit me like a warm soft wall. "Paddy broke his leg," I cried, yelling above the roar. "I'm sorry. We stayed too long and he broke it in a badger hole. The storm came and I couldn't leave him and I don't know if he's alive but I built a shelter and later a fire when

80

Nooking with Louise

the wind died down and he's down there now all covered
with snow—"

Dad jumped down and wrapped his arms around me in
the biggest hug I'd ever had. Mom climbed down with a
quilt in her arms. She threw it over my shoulders. "Eric, we
thought you were dead." Tears streamed down as she
touched my face. "Aren't you frozen?"

"You're a sight for sore eyes, boy," said Uncle George in
his big black snowmobile suit. "You okay?"

I nodded. I couldn't feel my feet though.

"What's the matter? You think we're all getting too much
sleep around here?" Norman laughed as he threw his arm
around my shoulder. "Better get into that cab and get warm."

But I couldn't. Not yet. "Paddy's down there," I said
pointing.

"He alive?" Dad asked.

"Yes. Maybe. I don't know." And then, "I think I killed
my horse."

"You get in the cab," said Mom. "I've got lots of blankets in there. We'll go check."

"No, no, I want to go." I grabbed a blanket from her.
"Come on."

Fear again, rising up, drowning hope, as I led them sliding down the side of the hill. Norm, his face grim now, with
a .303. We waded through the snow and into the little camp
that had been our world for the longest night of my life.
Paddy was just a snow-covered hump in a sea of drifts.
There was just a small, dark space between him and the
roof. Only the saddle, sitting oddly on its side, suggested
there was something there. I ran to Paddy and knelt down.

"Watch his leg," I said to Dad beside me. I brushed some
snow away. Dad grimaced when he saw the splint. Paddy's
head was covered. I gently brushed it off.

"Paddy? Paddy, boy. Wake up." His eyes, his ears, his

mouth were full of snow. Ice had formed around his nostrils. I brushed snow away from his eye. It stayed closed.

Oh Paddy, please, wake up, I prayed. I brushed the snow from his ear. And then, it twitched.

"He's alive!"

Paddy snuffled. A tiny beautiful sound. Then . . . he opened his eye.

I looked up. Four adults stood there, grinning, wiping tears from their eyes, Norm with the rifle by his side.

"You won't be needing that," I said. "I'm going to make sure of it."

Necking with Louise

I'D NEVER THOUGHT of Louise as beautiful. True, she sure wasn't hard to look at and none of us guys would have been ashamed to bring her home to Mom. If we did that sort of thing, which we didn't. No, Louise was more good-looking in a jock sort of way. Black curls always bouncing, brown eyes alive and eager as if she was just happy to be in on the joke. Louise was Polish, a big-boned farm girl. Her square shoulders made it seem like her bra strap was always about ready to snap. She was tall and had strong legs, and at every track and field meet she'd end the day walking around with five red ribbons flapping on her chest. But to me, Louise was just one of the girls in high school I thought of as a great kid, like a sister—only better. She'd be the first girl any of us would pick to be on our ball team.

I don't know when it was that I stopped thinking of her like that and started to think, you know, that she had possibilities. Maybe it was after I heard that Lenny Roberts had been out with her, had made the big trip to her parents' farm eighteen miles north of town and reported back that Louise Polonski was just a ferocious kisser. Or maybe it was that I was waking up to the fact that all girls didn't have to look like Anna-Maria, Miss Blonde & Beautiful. She'd been my first and only girl friend, and she'd dumped me three months ago for my ex-friend Peter. Or, then again, maybe it was just being with Louise in the gym equipment room that day after the girls volleyball game. It had been a house league match and I'd been referee. Louise had played like a demon. I was putting away the net when she came in with an armful of volleyballs. You'd think she'd just stepped out of the rain. Her black hair was glistening and flat against her face. Sweat poured off her and I could see little creeks of saltwater headed for the valley down the front of her jersey. She flashed a toothpaste smile and dropped an avalanche of balls into a cardboard box.

"Great game, Louise."

Another smile. "Thanks. We needed that one. They've been whipping us all season." She bent over a little, grabbed the hem of her jersey and pulled it up to wipe the sweat from her eyes. I noticed a little brown mole on her back, right side, just below her neck. It made me think of the morning star—I haven't a clue why—and it disappeared as she rose.

I grabbed at the whistle still around my neck, swallowed hard and tried to sound cool. "What are you doing Friday night? Want to go to a movie?" All the motion in that equipment room stopped. There was just the two us and the nets, balls, the smell of sweat and liniment—good smells. Those brown eyes did a quick check of my face, searching for something. I don't know what.

But then she smiled in a way that made everything inside just kind of get hot and prickly like a wool sweater. "Yeah, I'd love to," she said.

I laughed with relief. Gawd, I was grateful to this girl for making it so easy.

"What's playing?" she asked.

"*Dr. Zhivago.*" I had checked the poster in the town café just yesterday. "Omar Sharif's in it; I don't know who else."

"Oh, I like him," Louise said. She was standing very close. I could smell the perfume in the shampoo she used.

"Yeah, he's good." Why hadn't I noticed before how beautiful she was? "Why don't I pick you up around 6:30? We can grab a burger and shake before the movie."

Suddenly the room erupted with a furious jangling. The school bell. One was mounted on the wall just outside the door. Louise threw back her head and laughed, big white teeth framed by red lips rimmed by droplets. We waited until the bell stopped. "That'd be great," she said. "I look forward to it." She brushed by me, touching my arm with her wet hand. "Gotta hit the showers. See ya later."

I turned, walked out of the room behind her and watched Number 11 run down the gym and into the girls locker room. "I look forward to it," she'd said. I wondered who'd given her advice on how to make guys feel great. I walked down the gym to the boys locker room, whistled through my shower and went to class feeling happier than I'd been in months.

That was Wednesday. On Friday, a quarter past six, I was hurtling north to Louise's in my '58 Ford. I'd rushed home from school, washed and waxed my car, vacuumed my dog's hair off the seats and sprayed the inside with enough air freshener to make it smell like a lilac plantation. It was a clear spring evening; the crops just coming up stretched away from the road like green pool tables. Red-winged blackbirds perched on small willows by roadside sloughs, their red and yellow chevrons flashing in the setting sun. The car's shadow raced along in the ditch to my right and a long gold feather of dust hung over the road behind me. I pushed a freshly polished cowboy boot down on the gas. I didn't want to be late.

Louise's father answered when I knocked on their weathered back door. I had seen him before at hockey games or at the school. He was a shy man, older than my dad, with a nice smile and a heavy accent. We shook hands. Louise's mother came, too, wiping her hands on her apron. And then Louise's little sister poked her head around. Gawd. The whole family was there. I felt like an alien who'd just landed. This being Saskatchewan, we talked about the weather and how the crops looked. And just before we got on to the subject of rain, Louise appeared.

I never knew anyone could look so good in a T-shirt and jeans. She'd done something with her hair. I'd never seen it like that. It was . . . well, it was big. And shiny and black. And her eyes seemed bigger, too, and I realized later she had makeup on. Her T-shirt was white and tight and was tucked into her jeans, and she had a black leather belt with a shiny big buckle and black cowboy boots. That impressed me, too. Louise smiled and red lipstick filled the porch doorway and painted out the rest of the family. "Hi," she said.

"Hi," I answered. It seemed like a very little word and it just got lost out there in that farmyard.

Louise was easy to talk with. We'd driven the eighteen miles back to the highway and now it was another thirty-five miles to Riverside, the only town around big enough to have a real movie theater.

We were both nervous at first, even though we were in the same grade at school, different classes. But Louise put her left arm up across the seat and chatted away like we'd done this a hundred times already. And after a few miles I felt like we had. She laughed when I leaned over and opened the glove compartment to turn on the radio. "That's great," she said. "Where'd you get it?"

"It's from an old MG. Bought it from a guy for ten bucks."

"Sounds nice." She opened up the glove compartment

again to turn up the sound. I liked that. "King of the Road," Roger Miller's new hit song, was playing. She hummed along and I realized how good it was to have a girl in my car again. I let out a long slow sigh that she wouldn't notice and tapped my fingers on the steering wheel. And before we knew it we were in Riverside.

The Jade Garden Restaurant had the best burgers, and it's where the kids from our town always went after hockey games and before movies. We ordered, sipped our milk-shakes, and talked about teachers and final exams and summer jobs. Louise was going to work as a nurses' helper in a small hospital fifty miles away—the hospital where I'd been born as a matter of fact. I told her my uncle had gotten me a job driving bulldozers building irrigation dams in the middle of nowhere. In the back of my mind I was calculating the miles I'd have to put on to see Louise if I wanted to, and it was kind of depressing to think about, so I didn't. I paid the bill and we went to the movie.

Omar Sharif was Dr. Zhivago, an upper-class doctor from Moscow who was really a poet at heart. And even though he was married and had kids, he fell in love with Lara, played by Julie Christie. She'd been seduced by her mother's boyfriend, who was a real bad apple. The First World War broke out and Zhivago went off to the front, where the Russians were fighting the Germans. The land looked flat and empty—just like Saskatchewan. Zhivago and Lara ended up meeting near the front. She had become a nurse. They worked together patching up wounded soldiers in a filthy hospital. And that's when Louise grabbed my hand.

Well, she didn't really grab it. She just kind of slipped her fingers inside mine like she was crawling into a safe place. I never expected that and suddenly there were all these strange feelings in my body. Things I'd never felt with

Anna-Maria. My right hand was getting warm, and I thought to myself, *Oh gawd, guy, don't start getting sweaty on me now.* But I didn't.

Her fingers were surprisingly soft and small and I felt strong and really good. I squeezed her fingers a little and Louise looked at me and smiled and moved a little closer and leaned her head toward me.

The new rulers, the Bolsheviks, didn't like Zhivago's poetry. He was a romantic and there was no room for romantics in the workers' revolution. So he and his family escaped by train to Siberia to her family's summer home until the dust settled. There Zhivago ran into Lara again. She was now a librarian in a nearby town. They went back to her apartment and there was a real steamy love scene that made my mouth go dry. I wanted to swallow hard, but I didn't dare. At least not until Louise shivered. I put my arm around her and she snuggled in close. I tried hard to concentrate on the movie, but I couldn't. I was too aware of Louise. I got up my nerve and kissed her hair. She made a sound like a kitten. That was encouraging. I was very conscious of the hard arm of the theater seat between us and I wished it wasn't there, and for the first time, I was very glad my car didn't have a stick shift and bucket seats.

"What a sad ending," sighed Louise later as we drove out of town and headed for home. There was a fingernail clipping of a moon hanging on a blackboard sky. "I can't believe Lara and Zhivago never really got to be together."

"Yeah. I guess they just weren't meant to, eh? That's what makes it such a tragedy."

Louise looked at me. She was sitting close beside me. "You mean you think it was fate that kept them apart?"

Something in her question, in the way Louise held her head . . . I don't know . . . suddenly made me look at us as if from a distance and high above. I looked down and saw my car on the dark road with two long V's of lights probing the black ahead like some insect's antennae. From up there we looked very tiny in the great darkness of the prairies. And our lives seemed so insignificant. It was such a big feeling that it made me a little sad, like we were all alone out here on this planet and I was very lucky to be with this girl.

"Do you believe in fate or do you think we're all free to do what we want?" I asked as I put on the brakes.

"Why are we slowing down?" she asked.

I laughed. "Come on. You gotta answer the question." I checked the rearview mirror. There wasn't another car on the road. I pulled over and aimed for a crossing up ahead that went into a field.

"I don't know," Louise said. She was very serious. "I'd like to think that I'm the one making the decisions, but sometimes I think somebody or something else is. Maybe fate or God or whatever's got something planned for me, and I wonder sometimes when I'm going to find out." I turned the car into the crossing and stopped on the edge of a field of summer fallow. "Why?" she turned again to look at me with a hint of a smile. "Why'd you ask that?"

I turned to look at Louise and brought my hand up to her face. "Because I really can't stand the thought of going one more mile without kissing you," I said. Slowly I brushed the back of my fingers across her cheek and then pushed my fingers up into the hair behind her ear. Louise pressed her face into my arm and smiled and the green lights from the dashboard danced in her big dark eyes. "And I don't know whether you think it's me who wants to kiss you or that fate's making me do this"— she laughed as I leaned forward —"but I want you to know it's me."

It was at that moment I found out I didn't know a darned thing about kissing. And something else, too. I had watched Louise sip that milk-shake at the café and leave a red ring of lipstick on the straw. I had watched her talk and laugh, and I thought I knew what she was like—but I didn't. I discovered you can never tell what kind of a kisser a girl's going to be until you kiss her. It started out very soft and gentle. Our lips were like warm caterpillars crawling over each other, slowly exploring, touching, wandering and then suddenly it was like a storm came up and there was lightning and thunder and we searched for shelter and we crawled into the big wet caves of our mouths, which we found were delicious, so we sent our tongues out to search the caves and they went back and forth and wrestled and played and the caves kept changing shape. It was like a wild ride at the exhibition but all in slow motion. I felt like I'd fallen into the House of Pleasure and I couldn't quite believe it because I was finally inside and I couldn't get enough and I never wanted it to end. It seemed like half an hour went by, but it was probably more like five minutes. We stopped for air. We opened our eyes. The car windows were all steamed up. Both of us leaned back and laughed.

"Jeez," I said, "you're amazing."

Louise laughed again. "So are you."

I felt an incredible hunger, like I'd been starving and didn't know it until now. I leaned forward. "I want to do that again."

Louise held her watch up to the dashboard lights. "I can't," she said. "We have to get going. My parents worry about me driving so far so late."

My face must have shown my disappointment. She laughed again. "But once they know I'm home, it's okay."

It took a second to realize what she was saying. She wants more, too. I couldn't believe it. I turned to start my car. "Fasten your seat belt, girl," I said. "This is Gemini Four, Houston. We're setting course for the Polonski farm." Louise giggled and grabbed my arm as I shifted into reverse.

Once we got back onto the highway, Louise cranked down her window and turned up the radio. Then I put my arm around her and she squeezed so tightly up against me I could feel the softness of her breast. I imagined we were riding double on a wild stallion galloping through the night. The roads were so straight that I drove for miles with just my knee on the steering wheel. We kissed at forty, at fifty and sixty miles an hour. I grabbed Louise and put a headlock on her and held on until she cried uncle. We laughed. We sang, "It's been a hard day's night, and we've been kissing up a storm." The Beatles were rocking. We were rocking. I never imagined I'd be so excited about taking a girl home.

It was just after 1:00 when we crept slowly into Louise's farmyard. I stopped, not too close to the house. The yard light was on but the house was dark, except for one dim light in what I guessed was the kitchen. "Mom can relax now," said Louise. "The light will go off in a minute."

I turned to her and we came together like two magnets. There was nothing soft about this kiss. It was hard and fierce and we banged our teeth a couple of times and laughed without stopping. And in a minute my mouth was numb, like rubber, and I couldn't tell where my lips ended and hers began. And our faces were wet and I was hot and my feet were hot in my cowboy boots and my jeans were too tight. We squirmed, trying to push our bodies even closer. Louise was plastered against me, scrunched into my arms. I could feel her breasts on my chest. I could feel her bra strap under her T-shirt. I brushed my hands over it and I had this thought that Mrs. Polonski had probably cross-stitched a No Trespassing sign beside those funny little hooks on the back. It was right about then that the yard light went off.

We explored our lips, our mouths, our eyes, our faces and mapped every square inch with our tongues, with our fingers. Suddenly Louise grabbed my right earlobe between her teeth, licked my ear and then stuck her tongue inside. It could have been a cattle prod. It had the same effect. My body jumped into red alert. My heart was in overdrive. "You like that?" whispered Louise, her hot breath moving like a Chinook over my wet ear. I remembered calves licking milk from my fingers with their rough tongues as they learned to drink from a pail. That had been my only experience with tongues.

"Uhhumm."

She kept going, drilling into my brain with that wild, wet, writhing snake of a tongue. "Here," I said after a while, moving my mouth to her ear. "My turn." I discovered that night the art of giving and taking, the excitement of mutual pleasure with a girl. The kissing went on and on. It was a total immersion course. It was mouth-to-mouth resuscitation of my life. I had a girl friend again. And she was great.

Finally I pulled back and moved the wet hair away from Louise's face, tucking the strands behind her ears. "I like watching you," I said.

"You do?" She sounded surprised. "When?"

"Oh, when you're in the gym. You're feisty as hell."

She laughed. "I didn't think you even knew I existed." Her voice was soft and low in the dark. "I've wanted to go out with you for a long time."

"You have?"

"Oh yeah, but you were always hung up on Anna-Maria."

"Well, that's over and done with."

"You know something?" Louise asked.

"What?"

"I was at that final game against Rousseau. You're a beautiful skater."

"You were?" I was very pleased to know she'd been there. "Yeah, well, that was a tough game to lose."

"And you're feisty, too."

There was a teasing smile in her voice.

"Takes one to know one." And I immersed myself once again into a pool of hair and lips and skin.

It was almost 3:00 AM before I finally slowed down on the road by our farm and turned to go up the lane. My parents had just had it graveled and I was sure they'd done it so they could hear me coming home late at night. Our yard light was still on. I tiptoed up the steps into the porch and flipped the switch. Our beagle, Scamp, jumped up on me. His tail beat against the wall like a drum. "Shhhhhh. Come on, boy. Let's go."

He followed me out to the bunkhouse beside the garage. It's where I lived from spring until freeze-up, away from my two younger sisters and parents. There was no power so I'd run an electrical cord through the window from the garage for my radio. At night I often listened and read for hours. There was a potbellied coal-wood stove, my wrought iron bed, an old yellow hutch full of books, a small table and chairs. That was it. That was enough.

I stripped and jumped into bed under flannel sheets and an old quilt. I lay there in the dark, hands behind my head, staring into the blackness at the ceiling. I could smell Louise on my skin. I could taste her. My face still tingled. I closed my eyes and tried to replay every word, every sound, every touch of the evening.

Outside there was a chorus of crickets in the grass and bullfrogs slinging base notes from the pond and, drifting in on the warm night air, the yelping of coyotes down by the river. It was no use. I couldn't sleep. I got up and went out naked into the night. Scamp got off the bed and followed. The dark outlines of the barn and house, the trees, were small against the spattered blackness above. My head was full of sounds—the rustling of clothes, the smacking of lips,

Louise's whispers. I started to jog across the yard where we play ball, past the machine shed, the diesel tanks and out to the field south of the house. It was summer fallow and there was a damp carpet of soft green thistles just coming up. I broke into a run, Scamp right beside me. I ran like I'd never run before. Like a big buck deer, I ran. Like the deer who so easily clear the fence behind the barn, I leapt into the air. I ran southeast toward the end of the field where, above the trees, the constellation Orion, the hunter, ran across the sky with his dog, Sirius. Fueled by the kisses of Louise Polonski, I felt I could run forever.

The Summer I Read
Gone with the Wind

T HE SIGN SAID Office. The word was handwritten on a piece of white cardboard, wrapped in clear plastic and taped to the outside wall of the trailer. The plastic hadn't worked; rain had leaked in, smudged the ink and created light blue shapes like jagged lakes on a map. The door was jammed open with a piece of two-by-four and I could see a wooden desk inside. A set of muddy steel steps leaned against the trailer. I was just about to go up when a man appeared in the doorway. He was thin, his face as cracked and brown as an old baseball glove. The soggy stub of a roll-your-own clung to the corner of his mouth. He wore a faded Caterpillar baseball cap, khaki shirt and pants. His work boots, battered and muddy, were laced halfway up. He squinted at me in the morning sun.

"Hi, I'm looking for Pete, the foreman," I said.

"You found 'im." He paused, removed the cigarette with stained yellow fingers, stuck the tip of his tongue out just a bit, picked a piece of tobacco off the end of it, then spit to the side for good measure. "We ain't hirin' though."

Huh? Have they changed their minds? I cleared my throat. "I'm Eric. Eric Anderson. I'm supposed to start here today."

He squinted again, looked at me hard like I was some door-to-door Watkins man. "What'd you say your name was?"

I told him. "Randy Tilson's nephew," I added.

The lights went on. "Why the hell didn't you say so?" He looked down, scraped some mud off his boots on the doorsill. "We get five kids a day comin' in here, lookin' for work. They don't know squat 'bout nothin'. Come on in."

The office was crammed with wooden desks and chairs, relics from some old government building. Wood-grain paneled walls were plastered with *Playboy* centerfolds. A gorgeous blonde with huge snap-on boobs smiled from a tool company calendar. A drafting table stood against one wall. There were large topographical maps and plans on it, held down by a couple of flat rocks and a parallel ruler. Above it hung an old cow skull with black horns. The place smelled of mud, stale tobacco and a very recent fart.

"So what can you drive?" I was filling in the employment form Pete had given me. He sat down at a desk across from me and dipped into a green can of Sail tobacco.

"I dunno. All I've ever driven is farm trucks and tractors."

Pete rocked back in his chair, sprinkled shredded tobacco into a Zig Zag paper, rolled it back and forth with one hand, then licked the paper along the glued edge. He smoothed the wet edge down and, with a satisfied look, put the cigarette in his mouth. He fished a stainless steel lighter out of his shirt pocket, flicked it open, flipped the wheel with his thumb. The flame threatened to engulf his cigarette. I always liked the sharp smell of lighter fluid, but not today. Pete pulled on the cigarette, leaned back even further, blew a cloud at a faded Miss December. "Think we better start you off on the water truck till you get the lay of the land. Then, if you don't fuck up, maybe we'll put you on a cat."

He's dry and crusty as an old grasshopper. I didn't like him. It was going to be a long summer.

"Come on," he said, "I'll give you the cook's tour, then we'll get you to work."

The construction camp was a jumble of long white aluminum trailers—I counted nine—squatting on the prairie grass in a government pasture. We were surrounded by nothing but gophers. Not a building or tree in sight. It was hot already. The flat green horizon shimmered, foxtail grass swayed in the July breeze and mare's-tails swept across the milk-blue sky. Not far away, a killdeer sounded a warning, trying to lure a fox away from its nest maybe.

We walked toward one of the trailers. "We got a crew 'bout twenty-five, sleep in these four bunk trailers." He waved his hand, then pointed. "This one's yours."

The trailer was divided into three rooms. Mine was a beige rectangular box with a scuffed brown linoleum floor, two single brown iron beds with prison-gray blankets, a board shelf above each bed, a nearly collapsed metal folding chair and four-inch nails hammered into the wall for clothes. "Welcome to the Bailey Brothers summer resort for farmers' sons," Pete said with a laugh. In the pit of my stomach there was a knot tightening.

"That's Stan there." Pete motioned to my new roommate's unmade bed, pile of dirty clothes, crumpled cigarette packages and magazines. "He's a cat skinner. Knows everything there is to know about construction."

Doesn't know much about housekeeping. I threw my bag on the bed. I'd unpack later.

One of the trailers was for bathrooms and showers. Paper towels lay in puddles on the floor. A rainbow of cloth towels, some new, some faded and thin, hung on one wall. In the shower area there were waterlogged wooden slats on the floor. The place smelled of soap and damp and mold.

"So what grade you in?" Pete asked as we walked toward the mess trailer.

"Just finished ten." Grasshoppers zippered the air in front of us.

"How'd you do?"

"Not bad. Not great either. Seventy-eight average."

Pete motioned to a small brown trailer out behind the cookhouse, toward the rumbling sound of a diesel. "Generator. Runs night and day."

We stopped outside the mess trailer. "Lotta people here'd think those'd be pretty damn good marks."

"Yeah, well, my parents aren't too happy. They want A's. They think I play too much sports."

Pete grabbed a piece of crested wheatgrass, twirled it around his brown index finger, then stripped the top off with his thumb. "What do you think?"

"If it weren't for sports, I wouldn't want to be in school."

Pete threw the grass aside. "Then you're stupider than you look, kid." He glared at me. "I got my grade eight. And this is as far as that gets you."

My face went hot as Pete wheeled around and stepped up into the trailer. I followed like a spanked pup.

The cookhouse and mess trailers were joined at right angles in a T. The mess trailer had four long plywood tables covered with linoleum and edged with aluminum strips. The wooden benches on each side were painted dark brown with initials carved into the seats. A serving table held huge warming pans with leftover pancakes, sausages, scrambled eggs and fried potatoes. I hadn't seen so much food since the last fowl supper at church. A thin man in a white T-shirt and apron came out of the kitchen and picked up one of the pans. His skin was as black as good loam. I'd never seen a Negro so close up before.

"Hey, Gerry—meet our new truck driver." Gerry stopped, looked up, nodded. He had short hair in tight black curls dusted with white. It was hard to tell whether it was flour or he was just going gray.

"This is Eric." Pete looked at me, pointed at Gerry. "Gerry here's going to put some meat on your bones before the summer's through." Gerry smiled. "How's Lily?" Pete asked.

"Oh, she's fine, yes, she's jus' outside havin' a smoke after the mornin' rush, you know."

"Okay, see ya' later. Better get the kid here earnin' his keep." Gerry turned with his pan and went into the kitchen.

"Breakfast's at 6:30," Pete continued. "Be ready to go by 7:30." He motioned around. "There's always a fresh pot of coffee on and something to eat. If you're here after hours, don't make a mess. We take bag lunches out to the site. There's a half-hour break for lunch. Supper's at 5:30. The food's pretty good and there's lots of it."

Uncle Randy had told me that food and a paycheck were the best ways to keep guys on the job.

"Got any objection to workin' nights?" Pete glanced at me as we bounced over a prairie trail in his green half-ton. We were on the way to the dam.

I shook my head. "Nope."

"Good. We run two ten-hour shifts with time off for meals and maintenance." We kicked up a storm of dust on a trail that ran across the pasture. Pete slammed on the brakes and geared down to go through a small draw. "Each shift has three buggy drivers, someone on the push cat, grader, couple of cats pulling packers and a water truck—that's you. And a foreman. That's me. We got one of the Baileys here now—they're the owners from Calgary—so you gotta look sharp. He fired a truck driver on Wednesday for goin' over the edge of the dam. Could've rolled the thing and got himself killed. We don't like anyone messin' up."

Without warning the land gave way in front of us to reveal a shallow valley of grass and scrub brush about a quarter of a mile wide. There was a thin line of bushes meandering along the bottom, and here and there I could see water in a creek sparkling. But to our right the entire landscape had been ripped open. There was a long dirt bank stretching from one side of the valley to the other: the dam. It was maybe thirty feet high. Earthmovers bounced across the top, belching black clouds of diesel smoke. I watched as one, heavy with a load like a pregnant sow, slowed, lifted part of its hopper, and laid down a strip of fresh soil. Then it turned, tore back across the dam toward us and veered off to our right. "The borrow pit's over there," said Pete, pointing beyond the buggy to a cloud of dust. "We're diggin' the canal at the same time. It's where we're getting a lot of good clay. Stan your roommate is there on a D-9 push cat. He gets behind the buggies 'n' pushes them with the blade as they fill up so they can get a full load and power outta there."

"Just the thought of ramming a buggy full of dirt with a cat scares the hell out of me," I said.

Pete laughed. "Don't worry, kid. Your job'll be to drive the water truck back and forth and spray water on the soil they lay down. It packs better when it's wet, so the dam'll be solid and won't wash away. Or blow away." He chuckled at his little joke. "See those two cats pullin' those packers?" He pointed down to the far end of the dam. "You drive back and forth with them and pack and water that stuff."

"What's that guy doing?" I pointed to the grader moving slowly at an angle along the steep face of the dam.

"Oh, he keeps everythin' neat and tidy and straight. We got to build each layer level and he's there to do that."

He's like a sportscaster calling the play-by-play about moving dirt.

"There's the surveyors." There was a gray half-ton parked, a couple of guys in white hard hats leaning on the box watching the buggies. "This is a government job. They don' work for us, but they're part of the job."

I saw a big red Ford truck sitting at one end of the dam with a large water tank on the back. "Where do we get the water?"

"Right there." Pete pointed to his left. A trail I hadn't noticed before led down to the creek. "That's Blackfoot Creek. There's a pump there and a diesel to run it. You start 'er up and fill your truck when she's empty."

Pete ground the truck into gear. "Okay, 'nough of this bullshit. Can't make any money this way. Let's get that truck movin'."

It was noisy and dusty, and big machines, bigger than anything I'd been on, were bouncing and roaring and flying around. It looked like a battlefield. And right then all I wanted to do was head for home and get on something nice and safe and uncomplicated like a John Deere tractor.

★ ★ ★

Louise Polonski
c/o Mrs. Sarah McQuarrie
P.O. Box 95
Settlers Butte, Saskatchewan

Thursday, July 8/65
9:58 pm

Hi Sunshine!

Boy, I miss you! And it's only Thursday! I think about you a lot when I'm driving truck all day. How's it going at the hospital? Do you like Settlers Butte? It's bigger than Lashburg, so hopefully there's more to do there—but not too much more! Hope you got my first letter. I sent it into Brewster on Tuesday with Gerry. He's our Negro cook.

The Summer I Read Gone with the Wind

It's been a crazy week already. Two more guys got fired. One blew the engine on his buggy. He didn't see that the oil light was on. A cat skinner went over the side of the dam and that was it for him. Just the thought of going over scares the hell out of me. Pete, the foreman, is a tough old bird. He'd just as soon fire you as look at you. I sure don't want to get on the wrong side of him.

Mom and Dad, Nicky and Tracey-Lynn are leaving tomorrow for B.C. Lucky them! That water would look pretty good right now. We're roasting in these ovens they call trailers! I don't know how the cooks can stand it all day.

I found an old book in my trailer under the bed. Gone with the Wind. *Have you read it? It's all ragged and the cover's ripped off, but it's good. It's about this girl, Scarlett O'Hara (she's our age), who lives on a cotton plantation in Georgia. What a brat! All she can think about is marrying this wimp, Ashley. It takes place just before the American Civil War. Old Mrs. Carroll would be happy to know I might actually be learning something!*

It beats playing poker, anyway. That's what some of the guys here do every night. It's either that or go into Brewster and drink. One guy, Gus, the mechanic (gold tooth, bald as a billiard ball, grease and oil oozing out of his hands and arms) lost his month's wages Tuesday night. And he didn't even seem to mind.

Stan my room-mate's okay but he's got a major crotch-rot problem. He's always scratching and he leaves his dirty underwear lying on the floor. They used to be white but I won't tell you what color they are when I find them. (You probably see enough of that anyway.) I just kick the underwear under his bed and make sure I have my boots on. And then there are his work socks and sweat. The heat just cooks all the smells up together. I had to get the can of lilac air freshener out of my car. I guess you get the picture. Makes you won-

Necking with Louise

der about people, eh? Like what happened to their noses? One good thing is that it keeps the mosquitoes away. Hah!

Mom and Dad sent a Care package up with Uncle Randy and Aunt Lisa. So I've got my favorite bird shit cookies to gnaw on. They're made with stiff white stuff and corn flakes and look like they were dropped by a passing seagull. Dad also sent me the June issue of National Geographic. There's an article there about South Vietnam. Dad said the whole thing's a bunch of American propaganda. It's pretty scary, though, because the city of Saigon is like an island surrounded by Communist-infested rice paddies, and no one can tell a commie from someone who's not. Which is how the Reds can sneak in anytime and blow up Americans.

That's about it for now. Except that I miss you like crazy. I really miss those big brown eyes. I can't believe it's been only a week since the Lashburg Sports Day. The dance was fun, eh? So was the ride home!!!!! Gawd, I wish I could kiss you right now. I can almost taste that red lipstick. Mmm, makes me think of that wild tongue of yours.

There's no phone here, so I'll call you from town on Sunday— my day off. You can write me care of Bailey Brothers Construction, P.O. Box 44, Brewster. I can't wait to get your letter. I'm listening to the Beach Boys on a radio station in Nebraska. It's coming in clear as a bell on the skip.

X X X O O O
Eric the dam builder

★   ★   ★

Sunday, July 11, 1965

"This town's deader than a door nail." Chip cranked the wheel of his half-ton in disgust and turned off Main Street. We were cruising around Brewster, the small town closest to the dam. Chip was a buggy driver from Saskatoon. He was two years older than me. I had a feeling he was kind of wild.

"Looks like the Russians just bombed this place."

"Waste of a good bomb." We laughed.

It was Sunday. It was hot and sunny and we were bored stiff. There was nothing open and hardly a soul on the wide dusty streets. Chip fiddled with the radio, trying to find a station that didn't play Jimmy Reeves. We drove down a side street with worn wooden sidewalks and maples. A tiny mustard-yellow house had a white sign with a picture of a needle and thread and the name *Miss Pin-A-4*. I found something about that sign depressing.

"Let's go to the BA and get a Coke. Then I want to call Louise."

I fed a quarter into the coin slot on the cooler, slid the bottle along the metal rack to the gate and pulled. I popped the cap off with the opener on the side of the cooler, handed it to Chip and got another.

We sat down on the gray painted curb in front of the service station. It was closed. There was no one around. A dusty yellow dog was sprawled asleep in the shade by the door. Chip pointed with his bottle across the road. "There's a phone booth beside the hotel." He shook a bug out of his shoulder-length hair.

I felt the pocket of my jeans. I had enough change. Her number was written on my palm. I dropped two quarters and a nickel into the phone and the operator put me through.

"Hi? Louise?"

"Hi." She sounded tired, surprised.

"How are you?"

"Fine. Janet and I just got up. At least not too long ago. What time is it?"

"Two-thirty, lazy bones, a little after. Chip and I are in Brewster; he's one of the crew. It's our day off, but there sure isn't much doing around here."

"Yeah." She yawned. "So how's it going?"

"Great. If you call driving a big water truck back and forth all day great." It was stifling in the phone booth. I opened the folding door, jammed my foot up against it, took a sip of my Coke. Chip was getting into his truck. "I miss you, Louise."

"Yeah." A sigh. "I miss you, too."

"It's good just to hear your voice. You sound so warm and sleepy. I wish I was there right now instead of stuck here."

"I know. You seem so far away, too."

I imagined her in shorty pajamas curled up in a chair, legs tucked under her.

"Hey, guess what? This morning Pete, the foreman, told me they were ready to make a cat skinner out of me! I don't know whether that's good or what—the way they're firing people around here. I'll be on the night shift driving a big cat pulling a packer. But the really good news is—I've got three days off!"

"Great. When?" Louise sounded more awake. Chip rolled up beside the sidewalk with the radio blaring. I motioned for him to turn it down.

"Starting Thursday. I leave right after work. And I don't have to be back until Sunday at 8:00. What shift are you working? Can you get time off?"

"Straight days now. I have to work Friday, but we start at 7:30 so I'm off early. I can be home by 6:00."

"Great. Let's do something. What do you say?" Chip

honked and pointed across the street. Two girls were walking by the grocery store. They were sixteen, seventeen—it was hard to tell. The blonde waved. Her chunky friend with brown hair giggled. Chip nodded his head in their direction. I shook my head, let the door in the telephone booth shut.

"Yeah, maybe we can get some of the gang together, have a wiener roast." Chip honked again, this time at the girls. He waved. The brunette said something and they laughed loudly.

"Okay, great. Look, I have to go. But I'll call you just after 6:00 on Friday, okay?"

"That'll be good."

"The '58 Ford's goin' to be flyin' home!"

Louise laughed. I could almost see her white teeth flashing.

"Here's a big juicy kiss to do you until Friday." She laughed again at the long noise I made on the phone.

"Here's one back," she said.

I took it like a love-starved dog.

"Bye. Thanks for calling."

"Bye. Thanks for being there."

Stepping out of that booth was like getting out of a sauna. "No," I said to Chip as I got into the truck. "I don't want to chase those chicks."

"Ah, come on." He laughed. "How many miles away is she?"

"Too damn many." I drained the last of my Coke. It was warm as spit. "Let's go back, maybe throw the football around for a bit."

"Shit," said Chip as he took one last look at the girls walking away, then spun his tires in a U-turn. "She better be worth it, pal."

I wasn't listening; it was Friday already.

★　★　★

Wednesday, July 21, 1965

"Hey, you little bugger, how'd you know I don't have my .22?" The gopher squeaked, sat upright on the edge of his hole. His head jerked this way and that as he checked me out, then looked behind him, forepaws folded tightly against his chest. His tawny coat glowed.

"Just drinking my coffee. You're lucky this time, fella." I was sitting on a rock not far from the camp. The sun was high. It was 11:30. It had rained in the night, not enough to shut us down, but enough to make the prairie air clean and fresh. I'd had breakfast, then little more than a nap. After three nights of work, it was still hard to sleep during the day.

Another squeak. Another gopher's head appeared, smaller. She came out slowly and stayed low, behind her mate. "Ahh, good morning, miss. And what have you two been up to?"

I'd been thinking of Louise. A bunch of us had gone to a wienie bake Saturday night. Basically we sat around the fire and laughed. Louise was flying, telling stories about her patients. Some of them real characters like those two old Norwegians, Casper and Sigurd. She showed us Sigurd's imitation of a pickerel eyeing a fishhook. It was very funny.

Sunday was the best. Louise and I went for a swim, just the two of us down by the Sandy Coulee. There was no one around. "Race you to the other side," I yelled and dove in. We reached the shallows out of breath, laughing. I splashed her. Louise ducked, choked on the water. I watched it slide off her brown skin, glistening. We slipped back into the water like two seals and dove down. Louise came up behind me. She grabbed my shoulders, pushed herself against my back. Her breasts, arms, legs, warm and slippery against mine. I turned to laughing eyes, wet lips. We kissed, pressed ourselves together, wrapped our legs around each other and sunk down, down, until we could hold our breath no longer. We continued on my quilt, under the hot sun and blue sky. Cumulus clouds drifted by, white and fluffy as washday, with Frank Sinatra on the car radio. We kissed and kissed. By ourselves, in our bathing suits, we didn't dare do anything else. Leaving later was like pulling a rubber band, pulling slowly, sadly, until it snapped.

Good-bye. See you soon?

A shadow sped across the ground; the gophers squeaked —a high-pitched cry of alarm—and disappeared down their hole. A ground owl was hunting. I shaded my eyes and watched as it banked against the sun, swooped down and landed out of sight. *Must be living in an old badger hole over there.* I got up. My coffee cup was empty.

"Knock, knock," I said through the screen door on Gerry and Lily's trailer. A radio was playing.

Lily came to the door. "Well, hello," she said with a wink and a big fat grin. "It's the cat skinner. Come on in." She stood aside. "See you brought your mug." I stepped up into their trailer. We'd talked a couple of times before, usually in the evening, when they were on their steps. They had said to come over sometime.

"Gerry, bring the kid here some fresh coffee." Pete always called me The Kid. The name seemed to be catching.

"I can't sleep." I held out my mug as Gerry came over with a full pot.

"Well, this won' help in that direction." Gerry laughed as he poured out a coal-black stream of coffee. "How do you take it?"

"Just black, thanks." *Shit.* Saying that word around them made me nervous. Gerry didn't seem to notice.

"Have a seat." He motioned to a wooden kitchen chair.

"It's that generator mainly, and those blinds in my trailer don't keep the damn sun out, either."

Gerry sat across the small chrome and arborite table from me. Lily parked herself on a worn sofa. "And them mechanics always bangin' around, too," she added. Lily was a big woman. The sight of her in an orange flowered tent on the yellow tartan sofa was startling.

"Yeah. Oil Can Gus and Wild Willy," I said. They laughed.

Aside from the sofa and kitchen table, there wasn't much to their place. Just a wooden wardrobe, double bed, a black trunk with leather straps. A small red TV sat on two wooden Orange Crush boxes full of paperback books. I remembered seeing a small TV aerial on their roof. A paint-spattered transistor radio had music turned down low. "So, how d'you like drivin' cats?" Gerry asked.

"Old Pete's not exactly the world's best driver trainer." I slurped some coffee. It was delicious, had a chocolatey taste we never got in the mess coffee. "When I got back here Sunday, the cat was running and he said, 'Hop on.' We must've driven thirty feet. I'm not kidding!" Lily laughed and reached for a package of Camels on the windowsill behind her. "He showed me how to steer and how to put her in gear and use the brakes to turn and that was it! He jumped off and said, 'That's all you need to know, kid. You're on your own.'" Gerry smiled, got up, struck a match for Lily and held it to her cigarette. "I couldn't believe it. It's no wonder people are driving off the sides of dams and getting fired if that's all the help they get."

"Yeah, but you're forgettin' one thing, Eric." Gerry paused to light his own cigarette. Dropped the match in the empty beer bottle on the table; it had a couple of wilted brown-eyed susans in it.

"You're from a farm. You know about equipment an' stuff."

I shrugged. "Yeah, well. Anyway, there's really not much to driving a cat. We just go back and forth. In about two hours it was almost boring. Now the problem's staying awake all night."

"Yes, but aren't them stars out here so beautiful? And plentiful." Lily looked up like she was seeing them right through the roof of her trailer. "I never seen so many before in my life as out here."

"If you can keep your eyes open. The fan on my old cat blows all the heat from the engine back on to me so it's hot all night. And I'm not getting much sleep. Now, don't tell Pete this, but the second night, about four in the morning, I was driving standing up, trying to keep awake. Next thing I knew I was laying on the control panel. I'd fallen asleep."

Lilly gasped. "Goodness gracious Lord. Were you hurt, boy?"

I laughed. "No, I was fine. Good thing I didn't land on the tracks or you'd be burying me in a long flat box! That sure woke me up." Gerry shook his head.

A tin plate hung on the wall with a picture of the *Bluenose*. It said "Nova Scotia" along the bottom. I pointed to it, wanting to change the subject. "You guys go out there for a holiday?"

Gerry answered. "No, we're from there, originally at least. From Halifax. But there's no jobs there, so we been workin' out West several years now."

Lily cut in. "Ever heard of Africville?"

I shook my head. "It's a part of Halifax," Gerry offered.

"A poor part," Lily interrupted. "Full of colored folks from Halifax, from all over the Caribbean islands."

"I never thought there'd be . . . ah—"

"Negroes?" Lily laughed. "Go ahead, you can say it." I was sure my white face was beet red.

"Yeah." I swallowed, thankful she'd rescued me. "I didn't know there were so many Negroes down east. There sure aren't any in Lashburg."

Gerry laughed. "Oh, there's lots of us. Been there for years, too. Longer than many white folks who came from Europe, you know."

"His folks snuck up from the States by the underground railroad," continued Lily, "to escape slavery."

"My great-gran'daddy," said Gerry, "brought up his whole family an' he only had one leg."

"Tell him 'bout it," said Lily. Her eyes flashed. A cigarette ash fell on her dress; she brushed it off like a fly.

"Well, they were on a plantation in Georgia and he'd tried to escape and they caught him. With the hounds. And when they drug him back, the owner jus' walked up with his rifle and shot 'im in the knee. Jus' like that! All the other slaves were standin' aroun' and he said that'd be a lesson to 'em all. Couldn't get any medicine from the white folks, so they fixed him up with bush medicine. But they had to cut off his leg 'cause of the gangrene. He had such a hate on then that he jus' decided he'd be better off dead than stayin' in Georgia. So they escaped. Took 'em three months to get to Nova Scotia. And then they jus' about froze to death that winter." Gerry laughed.

"No, an' Halifax sure wasn't the Promised Land either," said Lily. A heavy sigh. She shook her head. "And now they're tearing Africville apart so black folks have to move into white neighborhoods. Urban renewal, they call it."

"I've been reading *Gone with the Wind*," I said, hoping to show that I wasn't completely ignorant of these things.

Gerry nodded politely. "That's a good story," he said. Lily heaved herself off the couch and shuffled over to the coffee pot.

"They had Negroes do everything, waited on them hand and foot, worked the fields. They even had kids, pickaninnies, who'd run out and hold the reins of white people's horses. I can't imagine living—"

"Shhh." Gerry held up his hand, turned to the radio on a shelf behind him. It was the CBC news. "Lord God Almighty!"

". . . the two churches, just outside Greensboro, Alabama, were wooden structures. They burned in minutes. . . ."

"Oh, my." Lily clasped her hands to her face. Gerry stared at the floor, listening grimly.

"Negro leaders say the fires are to intimidate Negroes and prevent them from registering as voters for the November elections. . . ."

"Of course they are," said Lily.

". . . and in Anniston, Alabama, the Negro man shot in the neck Saturday on a lonely highway has died. Willie Buxton was thirty-eight. He was shot from a moving car carrying four whites as he and several other Negroes were returning to their homes from work."

Gerry snapped the radio off. We sat in silence. I didn't know where to look. For the first time in my life I was ashamed of the color of my skin.

I thanked them for the coffee, went back to my trailer, and tried to sleep. But couldn't. I picked up a *Regina Leader Post* that Stan had been reading. On the front page was a picture of American soldiers in Vietnam running, carrying a bloody soldier between them. I noticed something about that photo. They were all Negroes.

★   ★   ★

Louise Polonski
c/o Mrs. Sarah McQuarrie
P.O. Box 95
Settlers Butte, Saskatchewan

Good morning Louise,

Necking with Louise

It's Monday, July 26, about 3:30 in the afternoon. I just woke up and I'm sweating buckets. I had an awful dream. I was in Vietnam, in the middle of a battle in the jungle, and a Vietcong tank ran over me. I was screaming; my legs were crushed. They looked like spaghetti and meat sauce. Then a big helicopter landed and you were in it. You were a nurse with a team of medics and you had this bright red lipstick on. You came over and looked at me. But you just shook your head and said to this guy, "He's a goner." And then you and the other medic picked up somebody else and headed for the chopper. I raised myself up and called but you didn't hear me. You all got into the chopper and took off. Shit, it was awful.

I woke up. The damn generator was rumbling, truck doors were slamming. I feel like hell. Who's this guy, Tony? You mentioned him three times in your letter. It was on my bed when I got back this morning. Are you going out with him? I'm feeling so far from you right now.

To top it all off, Chip's gone. He broke his arm so his football chances are shot, too. He crashed his buggy into another one. It wasn't his fault. The buggies have electric steering and they think some dust got into the system and it stuck. The damn thing just turned and rear-ended another buggy. Chip didn't have his seat belt on and he got thrown out. He's lucky. He could have been run over. He was the only other young guy around here.

Got a post card from Mom & Dad. They're having a great time, as usual.

Guess I better go have a shower. I'll call you Wednesday night.

Hugs
Eric

★　　★　　★

Monday, August 2, 1965

"Hello, Mrs. McQuarrie?"

"Yes?" She had a frail grandmotherly voice.

"Hi. This is Eric."

"Eric?"

"Yes, Eric Anderson. Louise's friend, from Lashburg."

"Oh, Eric." She laughed. "I'm sorry. The batteries must be going on my hearing aid. I'm not hearing so good today."

I heard her clock chime. Louise and I had had a fight on the phone the other night. *Our first fight.* I'd been torn up about it ever since. "That's fine. Is Louise there?"

"Louise, yes she's fine."

"No." Louder and slower. "Is Louise there?"

"Oh no, dear. They're out. They've got ball practice tonight. Tony just picked them up a few minutes ago."

Tony! That's who we'd fought about. *Why isn't she there?*

"Do you know what time they'll be back?"

"Back? No, I have no idea." She laughed. "I just can't keep up with you young people coming and going at all hours, always up to something."

At least someone's having fun. "Well, will you tell her I called?"

"Oh yes, I will. I'll be sure and do that."

"By the way, do you know if she got my postcard?" *You're seizing at straws, bud.*

"Oh, I don't know, dear. I just put all the girls' mail on the hall table here. I don't know. I don't recall seeing any postcard."

"That's okay. Thank-you very much, Mrs. McQuarrie. Please tell her I called."

"Yes, I'll do that, dear. Nice talking to you now. Good-bye." She hung up.

"Good-bye," I said to the dead receiver in the Brewster telephone booth.

★　★　★

Sunday, August 8, 1965

Huge drops of rain shattered in tiny explosions on the windshield. I turned on the wipers, leaned over, opened the glove compartment and turned up the radio.

"*Other arms reach out to me,*" I sang along with Ray Charles. "Georgia On My Mind" was one of my favorite songs.

"*Other eyes smile tenderly, still in peaceful dreams I see, the road leads back to you.*"

I was headed back to the Bailey Brothers camp. It was late Sunday night. The highway was ink-black and slick with rain, my windshield smeared with wet dead bugs.

I'd spent the weekend hanging out with Chip in Saskatoon, driving around in his red Galaxy 500 convertible! Brand new! His dad and mom just gave it to him. It was compensation for getting his arm broke. And for missing football. Must be nice.

"*Georgia. Georgia.*" It was not the radio squawking. *Gawd, I wish I could sing.*

Chip's parents owned a clothing store and lived in a huge stone house near the university. They had a pool in the backyard. That's where we spent most of the weekend. His sister, Lisa, was an A&W carhop, so we went by and fueled up on Grandpa burgers and root beer a couple of times. Chip's mom was up at their house in Waskesiu for the summer and his dad went up for the weekend. They left a well-stocked liquor cabinet behind.

"*No peace, no peace I find—just an old sweet song . . .*"

I found out I sure don't like scotch. And bourbon's

bloody awful. Rye and Coke with lemon's okay. We just hung around the pool today, feeling a little the worse for wear. I wish Louise could've been there. In her black bathing suit, all wet and warm.

I pulled into camp. After being in the city, I thought it looked ugly as sin. The dingy trailers glowed like old bones in the dark. I went into the bathroom trailer to brush my teeth. There was water running in the showers, but it didn't sound like anyone was in there. I went to shut it off.

Damn. Someone was laying in the bottom of the shower with all his clothes on.

"Hey, you okay?" No answer. Steam billowed out. I reached in, turned the water off and bent down. It was Stan. He reeked of booze.

"Stan." Still no answer. *Someone dumped him in here.* "Come on, let's get you out." I tried to lift him but he was too heavy. I dragged him out of the shower and laid him on the wooden floorboards.

Oh, Stan. He stunk to high heaven. It wasn't just the booze. He'd shit himself. Puked all over, too. "What a mess." *Welcome back.*

Stan groaned.

"Well, at least you're alive," I said.

I had to get those clothes off him. Wet, they were hard to unfasten; it was like wrestling with a dead man. I threw his stuff in a corner, dragged him back into the shower.

"Don't expect me to soap you down, you stinking old bugger." I turned the water to warm, then after a minute to cold.

Stan groaned with the shock of it, opened his eyes, blinked, tried to focus. Then squeezed them shut against the bright lights in the trailer. He looked very old and white and fat.

"Come on, let's get you to bed." I shut the water off, grabbed under his arm and lifted. Stan opened his eyes again, but not like he was seeing anything. He rose shakily. I threw his arm over my shoulder. He sagged against me, wet and shivering. We staggered down the steps into the dark.

It was still raining lightly. I half-dragged, half-walked Stan barefoot and naked across the trampled grass to our trailer. He didn't quite make it. Outside our door, he stopped, bent over and deposited what was left of his guts into the five-gallon pail we kept there for garbage. Then he crawled up the steps on his hands and knees, bare ass in the air.

I laughed grimly. "Now there's a sight to remember."

Stan climbed into bed and crumpled like a tent. I pulled the blankets out from under him and covered him up. He was shivering; his hands were shaking.

"Ohhhhh." Stan started to cry, then mumble.

"What?" More mumbling. I bent over him. "Stan, I can't understand you." His face was buried in the pillow. "Go to sleep, for chrissakes. I'm tired. I want to go to bed."

"K–k–kid?" Stan rolled onto his side, cradled his head in his arm. He mumbled something more. ". . . wife . . . 'n' kids . . ."

Shit. I came over, cleared the junk off his folding chair, pulled it closer to his bed. "I can't understand you. What are you trying to say?"

He roused himself a little. "I . . . I . . . I owned an outfit like this oncesh, me an' a couple of other guys. Ten years ago. You prob'ly find tha' hard ta b'lieve." He stopped, snuffed, wiped the snot off his nose. Left a streak of it on his cheek. "We were up north on a job. The phone rang—" His voice wavered. He started to cry, pushed the words through his sobs. "My wife. Kids. Dead. House burned to the ground. I didn't know what to do." His voice trailed off as he dropped his head. His shoulders shook. I sat still as a post.

"It's okay, Stan. Go to sleep. You can tell me in the morning." I went to pull the covers up farther.

"No, no, no." He waved me down. "Stay." I sat back on the chair. "I was los', totally fucked up. I always drank, but I jus' got drunk and stayed that way for 'bout six years." He looked up at me. "Los' everything. Everything I ever cared about. I jus' lost heart. Never did get it back. Even though I joined AA. And now . . ." He paused, stared off at nowhere in particular. "Now I'm jus' puttin' in time here."

He stopped, pulled up the covers, squirmed into them like a little boy. "Ya find out who your friends are, kid. Bailey boys said they'll always haf a job for me 's'long as I want." Stan turned to me, blinking. "You're smart, kid. Don' shake your head. Yes, you are. Jus' don' go an' piss your life away, tha's all." I was stabbed by the regret in his watery red eyes. He blinked, closed them then and fell asleep. Passed out more like it. Snoring.

I sat there for a long time listening to rain on the roof. I wasn't tired anymore. I got into bed, opened my book and, as war raged between the States and wounded soldiers filled up hospitals and train stations, I fell asleep.

★   ★   ★

August 13, 1965

Louise Polonski
c/o Mrs. Sarah McQuarrie
P.O. Box 95
Settlers Butte, Saskatchewan

Hi Louise,

I still haven't heard from you. I'm having a tough time understanding what's happening. I feel like you and I are so great together. You were becoming my best friend. Am I wrong? I feel crazy for even asking. It sure would be great to see you again—soon. I real-

ly hope you write. But the fact that you haven't means you're try-ing to tell me something. I just wish we could talk but I keep miss-ing you every time I call.

Nothing's making much sense to me these days. The whole world's kind of crazy. They're rioting in Chicago and Los Angeles. Commies and Yanks are slaughtering each other in Vietnam. Whites and blacks are shooting each other in the US. The Ku Klux Klan even burned a cross in Amherstburg, Ontario, for crying out loud!

Anyway, Dad and Mom are back. They had a great time. I'm going home to the farm next weekend to help get the combine ready for harvest. It means the summer's almost over. I can't even think about school. Football, yes. Homework, no.

Well, this is just a short note. Gotta go skin a cat. Miss you like crazy.

Eric

P.S. Holy Cow! I just heard on the radio. Seven thousand Negroes rioted in Los Angeles last night. Dick Gregory, the comedian, was shot and lots of people are dead! What the hell's going on down there anyway?

★   ★   ★

Saturday, August 14, 1965

Crack! The five ball shot in a blue streak past a herd of reds. Th-thunk. Corner pocket.

"I can see that yer youth hasn't been misspent entirely."

I looked up. It was Pete, grinning.

"Hi, how you doing?" He had his hat off, thin gray hair

slicked back over his farmer tan. He'd showered and was wearing clean clothes. I wasn't used to seeing him like that.

"Came in ta get my ears lowered." He nodded toward Albert, the barber. We were in the Brewster Pool Hall & Barber Shop, the busiest place in town on a Saturday night, next to the hotel beer parlor. Albert, bald head framed by his green visor, had a customer, was chatting away as he snipped, scissors flashing like punctuation marks. A bare bulb hung on a frayed cord above them. Colored bottles of hair tonic lined up against the mirror.

I was shooting pool with Gord and Duff, a couple of guys from camp. Duff went to have a leak. Gord was waiting, leaning against the wall by the scoreboard, chalking up his cue. I hadn't talked much with Pete, even after all this time at camp. Just tried to stay out of his way and do my job.

I walked around the table, looking for a red-ball shot. I didn't know what to say to him.

"So, it was a good week." It came out more as a question than anything.

"Was till 'bout 5:30 today," Pete growled. I looked up, surprised. "Frank quit. Got his paycheck and said tha's it. Stupid fucker left, jus' like that."

Frank was a cat skinner, pulled a packer on night shift. I hadn't known him really. Hadn't liked him much.

I found a shot, motioned with my cue. "One bank to the side." Clack. Thunk. Thunk. Thunk. "Damn it all to hell!" The red ricocheted around like a pinball. Pete laughed.

"Well, it appears yer a better cat skinner than a pool player after all."

Enjoying your night out?

Gord circled the table, grumbling about his poor leave. Duff was back, talking to the guys at the next table. I took out a stale wad of gum, tossed it into a tobacco can full of sand and butts and bottle caps that was nailed to the wall.

The ashtray. I peeled a fresh stick of Juicy Fruit, popped it into my mouth, offered one to Pete.

"No, thanks." His face went serious. "Got a favor to ask."

Pete! Asking me a favor? "Sure, shoot."

"I need you back on night shift." He paused. "To replace that asshole." Another pause. "Startin' tomorra' night."

Shit. So that's what this is about. And just two weeks to go. I thought of the trouble I had sleeping during the day, of staying awake all night, missing sunlight.

"I need a good farm boy out there. And you know how to handle equipment. Not like these other jokers who keep fuckin' up, breakin' things or jus' takin' off."

Wow. He thinks I'm doing a good job! I looked around to see if Duff and Gord were listening. They were. I smiled, suddenly felt taller, older even. "Sure, Pete. No problem. Be glad to."

"Good," he said. "Thanks." He glanced over at Albert. He was shaking hair out of his apron onto the floor. His customer was leaving. "Well, gotta go get ma beauty treatment," he said, laughing, and walked away.

★   ★   ★

Thursday, August 19, 1965

Clouds of black dust swept and swirled around me. Lights from the buggies bounced up and down, in and out of the dust. They wove, swerved, turned in flashes of yellow and disappeared, giant bees in an eerie dark dance. The night wind was cold, from the north, carried a touch of fall in it. Even with my jacket, I shivered. The coffee helped. I hunkered into my seat, steering back and forth along the narrowing top of the dam. My watch said 4:01 AM. *Another hour and a half.* There were a million stars out, a pale lightness in the east where the sun would rise.

This big D-8 was newer than the cat I'd driven before. Much easier to drive, with steering handles on the console instead of big levers to pull. The turning brakes were easier, too. You didn't have to tramp on them so hard. There was a big dozer blade on the front. Every now and then, to relieve the boredom, I'd lower it and practice smoothing out rough spots before I rolled over them with the packer. Nights weren't so bad anymore. The bosses weren't around much, so we were on our own. I knew what I was doing, too, and I never got tired of looking at the stars.

A horn honked. It was Gus. In the mechanics' truck, driving alongside. He waved, motioned for me to stop. I shifted into neutral, pushed the throttle lever down a little to let the diesel engine cool gradually. Gus, in his grease-black coveralls and welder's cap, climbed up the cat tracks, a big aluminum thermos in his hand.

"Hi, kid. How's it goin'?" He smiled, his gold tooth flashing like a meteorite.

"Fine. Cold though."

"Freeze the nipples off a witch's tit," I laughed.

He leaned over, looked at the control panel. "Temperature okay?"

"Yup, no problem." I'd just checked. I'd been told to do it every few minutes.

"She was runnin' a little hot today. Jus' wanna keep an eye on 'er. Coffee?"

"Love some. Just finished the last of mine."

Gus unscrewed his thermos. "It's got milk and sugar."

"I don't care," I laughed. "As long as it's wet and hot."

Gus perched a cheek on the gearshift box. "Cheers," he said as we raised our cups and drank. The coffee was sweet and thick, but I wasn't complaining.

Gus looked around. "Won' be long . . . summer's almost over." We could see the lights of the other cats, the water truck; one buggy was dumping its load, another right behind him. "Goin' back to school, I guess, eh?"

"Yup," I nodded, took another sip. "Grade eleven."

Gus nodded. "Gotta girl friend waitin' for you, too, I bet."

Ouch. I swallowed my coffee. "Well," I began slowly with a deep breath, "thought I had one. But she's been away this summer working." I stopped, looked for some words. "I don't know. Haven't seen her in weeks. Doesn't write. I can't get her on the phone."

I stared at the gauge lights, glowing circles. "It hasn't been a great summer that way."

Gus didn't say anything. Warmed his hands on his cup. A buggy roared by. Finally he spoke. "Look kid, if you don' min' me saying so, there's one sure way you can tell if a girl likes you. And that's if she's with you." He turned to me. "You know, hangin' out with you, goin' places, doin' stuff. Laughin', havin' a good time. If they ain't there, they just ain't there. That's all there is to it."

I forced a smile. It was good to talk to someone about it. I just never thought it'd be Oil Can. "Min' if I give you one more piece of advice?" I shook my head. "You can always tell if it's workin' by askin' yourself one little question: 'Are you happy?' If you ain't happy, it ain't workin'."

He made it sound so simple. *Was it really?* "You married, Gus?"

"Twenty-five years next month. Two girls an' a boy. In Saskatoon. The wife works for a vet. Oldest girl's in university. Costin' me a fortune." He laughed, an easy contented laugh. "Anyhoo," said Gus, his voice brightening suddenly. He slapped his knee. "It's jus' too beautiful a night to be lovesick over some silly-assed girl who doesn' know what's good for her. Look." He pointed to the sky. "Jus' like them stars, there's a million girls out there an' one's jus' waitin' for you." I laughed, freely now. "I see the old black queen's rising right up there." Gus had his head cranked back, looking straight up.

"What are you talking about?"

"Cassiopeia. Don't you know her, kid?" I shook my head. "You mean to tell me you're a farm boy, been raised under this panoramic view half the hours of your life an' you don' know what's even up there?"

I grinned. "Well, I know the Big Dipper . . . Little Dipper over there." I pointed. "Orion, he's my favorite. The hunter. And Sirius, his dog."

"So where's Cassiopeia then, if you're so damn smart." He was having fun.

"Haven't got a clue."

"That's what I thought. Look." He pointed. "See the North Star? Straight up. She's just a little over from there. Like a W. See? Right there."

"Oh, yeah." I was pleased to discover this.

"Well, she's married to Cepheus. That's him over there. King of Ethiopia." Gus talked straight up into the sky, like he was pointing out guests at a wedding. "And that's their daughter, Andromeda, jus' between her mom and the North Star. See it?"

"Yeah, I think so."

"Old Cepheus, he went with the Argonauts on their search for the Golden Fleece. And Cassiopeia there, she was vain as any woman, claimed to be more beautiful than all the sea nymphs. So the gods punished her, made her circle the pole upside down, forever and ever."

"Gus, how do you know all this stuff?"

"Know the town hall in Brewster?"

"Yeah?" I wondered what that had to do with anything.

"Well, there's a library upstairs, my frien'. Jus' full of books. And so I got myself a library card, seein' I was here for the summer."

How many times have I driven by that building?

"Oh sure, I gotta tie one on with the boys once in a while, let off some steam, but the res' of the time, I just lose myself in good books. Otherwise I'd spend all my damn money, and the wife'd have my knackers nailed to the wall quicker 'n' a shake of a dog's tail."

"Jeez," was about all I could say for myself.

"Ol' Oil Can surprised you, eh?" He laughed.

I snapped my head around, looked at him. It was too dark to see his greasy face. *How'd he know my nickname for him?*

"Oh, yeah, it's a good name, kid. Told the wife. Hell, you even got her callin' me that now." He laughed, held up his thermos.

"Sure, just a splash, if you got enough."

"There's always enough, kid. Of everything. You jus' have to know where it is an' go get it." He laughed, punched me on the shoulder and climbed down.

"Thanks, Gus," I called. "See you at breakfast."

He waved and was gone.

★   ★   ★

POSTCARD

Louise Polonski
c/o Mrs. Sarah McQuarrie
P.O. Box 95
Settlers Butte, Saskatchewan

Aug 19, 1965

Dear Louise,

Got your goodbye letter today. Guess I could see it coming a mile away. When you told me about Tony, it felt like someone had died. Wish I could say, "Well, frankly my dear, I don't give a damn." But I do. It'll be hard to be just friends, but I'll try. Guess I'll see you at school.

Eric

★   ★   ★

Saturday, August 21, 1965

The dance floor was jam-packed. We stood in one place and moved elbow to elbow with everyone else. A glass ball covered with mirrors rotated on the black ceiling above us, shooting beams of light everywhere. I'd never seen one before, except on TV.

"How do you like the band?" Lisa yelled in my ear. We were at The Embers, a restaurant and club at the east end of Saskatoon. Chip was dancing with Paula. It was louder than a couple of D-8's.

"They're great. It's good to be out. Haven't done this all summer." I was feeling good in my new leather jacket, new shirt and jeans. My face was tanned. It was nice to be clean.

Lisa grabbed my shoulder, put her mouth against my ear. "The lead singer works at CKOM just cross the street. He's a DJ."

I looked at the skinny guy with the long blond hair. "Oh yeah? What's his name?"

"Kenny Sebastian."

"Oh, I know him. Hear him all the time. He's good."

She nodded. We danced for a bit. Lisa and Chip had the same coloring: blonde hair, green eyes. They looked like brother and sister. Were friends, too. I envied that.

"Are you done soon at the A&W?" I yelled. Kenny had the mike stand bent over halfway to the floor. The lead guitar player was on his knees. I had no idea what they were singing.

"Friday." She took a couple of beats. "But I'll work part-time all winter. Won't be as much fun though."

"Yeah, I'm done Friday, too. Going home to help harvest."

Lisa was wearing a tight pant suit, bell bottoms, a white shirt with no bra. The puppies wanted out. She looked me in the eye. "So, what do you think of Paula?"

Her question took me by surprise. "Oh, she's nice." I didn't know what else to say.

"Well, she likes you." Lisa's eyes flashed. She smiled. "You should ask her out."

"W . . . Well," I stammered. Chip and Paula had gone back to the table, were drinking their Cokes.

"Chip said you broke up with your girl friend, right?"

"Yeah, well, she kind of dumped me. I just got her letter two days ago." I laughed.

"So ask her out," she said.

Jeez. Doesn't a guy get time to sort things out a bit first?

Her eyes danced. "Oh, go on! She's really neat."

"I know that." I did, too. I liked her. She was cute, long sandy-brown hair, soft hazel eyes. What I liked best was, she was funny, too, in a gentle sort of way. *Funny like Louise.* I saw red lipstick, those hungry lips, felt her wet kisses. *Shit.* The pain was there and then it was gone. It took me down a notch, not enough though. Lisa had her hands on her hips. "Okay, okay, I will," I said, with a laugh.

Paula was alone at our table watching the band. "It's a slow one," I said. "Want to dance?"

★   ★   ★

The Summer I Read Gone with the Wind

Friday, August 27, 1965

"So that's about it, eh kid?" Gerry smiled as he set down a huge pan heavy with hot steaming steaks. The mess trailer was full of guys chowing down supper like a pack of wolves.

"Yeah, I thought 5:30'd never come. Been waiting for Pete to sign my check."

"Gonna eat?"

"Nah, think I'll hit the road. It's a long drive." I'd packed this morning, slept like a log. *Finally!* I just wanted to get home.

He put out his hand. "Can't talk now, but it sure was a pleasure knowin' ya. Good luck with yer schoolin' an all."

"Thanks, Gerry. You guys have been great."

"Now don' you go sneakin' off without seein' Lily at the back door. She's got a li'l somethin' for ya to take home."

"Sure. Take care now."

"You, too."

I turned, wondering what would happen to them. I knew they were going up north this winter to cook in a logging camp. It was weird saying good-bye to people I'd probably never see again.

Lily was sitting on the steps outside the kitchen trailer, smoking. She rose, handed me a square package wrapped in tinfoil. "It'll tide you over till you get home to yer mama's cookin'.

It felt soft and heavy. "What is it?"

"Potato cake, darlin'. An ol' family recipe. I don't want you goin' and gettin' all skinny on me now that you won' have Lily's scrumptious cookin'."

We laughed. She gave me a hug, soft like a big feather pillow. Smelled of perfume and cooking oil.

A horn honked. We both turned.

It was Pete in his truck. He slowed down, waved, then yelled. "Check's in the office on my desk. Gotta go. Problem at the site." He waved again and drove off.

Shit.

Lily must have sensed my disappointment. "He doesn't like good-byes, tha's all, kid."

"Neither does Stan. He just slipped away this morning, too."

She didn't say anything. I couldn't think of anything either. Besides, I had this lump in my throat.

I went around the trailer, headed for the office.

"Hey, Eric." It was Gus. "Can I hitch a ride into town with you? Some of the guys are in there already."

"Sure, I'm leaving now."

"Not without this, I hope." He handed me an envelope. My check. With a big greasy thumbprint on it.

My car was covered with a powdery layer of dust. *That'll blow off soon enough.* Gus got in the passenger side. I opened the back door, unzipped my bag.

"Here." I handed him *Gone with the Wind*. "Finished it a couple of nights ago. It's good. Took me all summer to read the thing."

Gus looked at the dog-eared pages, the coffee stains and fly specks on the front pages.

"You read it or run over it?" We laughed. "Thanks."

I started the car. It bothered me, Pete just driving off like that. Something made me pick up the envelope.

"Better check this first, make sure they didn't short-change me."

I tore it open. There *was* something wrong with the amount. It was way more than it should have been. Five hundred dollars more.

I whistled. There was something else, a note, folded.

You did good, kid. Here's a little bonus from the Bai-
ley Brothers.
   Thanks for chipping in. Call us in Calgary next
spring. We may have a job for you. All the best.

   Pete

The writing suddenly went all blurry. Gus coughed,
rolled down the window. I blinked, coughed, too.
   "That crazy bugger," I said with a grin, handing Gus the
note.

The River

I T DRIFTED ALONG in the muddy water, turning lazily in the current, a little island of dirty yellow foam whipped up by wind and waves. It looked like the stuffing out of some old tractor seat. Or it could have been the meringue on a lemon pie abandoned long ago in the café window of some ghost town. The foam drifted down toward me, toward the cork bobbing on the line at the end of my fishing pole. Like a knife, the fishing line sliced through the foam as if it weren't there. The meringue simply rejoined and floated away. And I thought of Dad and his leg.

"You haven't even talked to him about it, have you?" Mom had said this morning, her green eyes firing accusations. I had shaken my head.

"Don't you know he could lose his leg?" She had tried to control her anger—or maybe it was fear—but it shook itself out of her and came right at me.

"He signed the papers, you know. If they can't get all the cancer, they're going to amputate." She had started to cry and the words came out in chunks between her sobs. "That'll be the end of the farm. And you act like you don't even care."

The foam was now a dot far downstream. The pus oozing out of the sore on Dad's right calf was yellow, too. For a long time, he thought it was just a boil or an infection, but it hadn't gone away. It's true, I hadn't thought about the farm. All I could think of was the river.

Every summer since I was old enough to help, Dad and I had fixed fence in the pasture down by the river, where we kept the cattle. It was hot dusty work digging fence posts, stringing barbed wire. At the end of the day, we'd strip naked, have a swim and then sit and talk before we gathered up our tools and headed home.

One time Dad took me to a ravine full of poplar trees and showed me where Grandpa and Grandma had camped during the Dirty Thirties. There had been no crops and no jobs, so they brought the cattle and horses and chickens down and fished and swam all summer. In the dark coolness of the ravine, they'd pitched their tents and built an ice-house. The old weathered boards were still there, all covered with green moss. I had lifted the rotting trapdoor with its cracked horse harness hinges and looked down into the pit where they'd kept the milk and eggs and homemade bacon. I went there many times after that and always wished I'd lived back then.

It was Sunday, late in September, and it was hot—Indian summer. Mom and my sisters had gone up to Saskatoon to visit Dad. He'd waited till harvest was over and the crops were in the bin before going into the hospital. I'd stayed home to milk the cows. My cousins, Jim and Barry, and I had come down to the river for goldeye. Someone said they're a delicacy in fancy restaurants in Winnipeg and I was always pleased we could get them for the price of a grasshopper.

We were fishing near the bridge, a big black CN Railway bridge with crisscross girders that sprawled half a mile across the river on five concrete piers. The railway tracks were on top of the bridge and underneath was for cars. We often watched long freight trains rumble over, counting boxcars as they rolled by. Sometimes there were flatcars with new red or green tractors and combines. The best ones, which came in late summer, had double-deckers with new cars from factories down east.

On Sundays we drove down the khaki hills and across the bridge to the town park on the other side. The thick groves of tall cottonwoods and maples were an oasis away from the blast furnace of the prairie. Everybody came to the park. After our picnic lunch we kids would run wild all day in the hills while the adults played horseshoes or visited or slept on blankets in the shade. And in the evening when it was time to go home and none of us kids could be found, our parents called using their car horns to honk out the patterns of our phone numbers on the rural party lines. Our family's signal was two long rings and three short ones. And when those horns echoed through the river hills, we stopped and listened and were always relieved when the signal wasn't ours.

"I'm going to try down there a bit," I said to Jim. He'd just walked up with a disgusted look on his face. I motioned in the direction the foam had gone.

"Better take some more of these." Jim handed me a Coke bottle with a cork in it. He was fifteen, a year younger than me, with a face full of freckles and sandy red hair. He was always kind of nervous and I figured he was skinny because he burned off calories just standing still. I took the cork out and shook the bottle. Five or six live grasshoppers came out into my hand. They were covered in the tobacco juice they spit out when they're cooped up like that.

I stuffed them into a plastic bag. "No luck up there?"

"Not a nibble."

"Where's Barry?"

"Oh, he's having a dump in the weeds. The guy's got the runs from eating too many chokecherries." We laughed.

Barry was a year younger than Jim, round like his name, more laid back.

I took off my running shoes and socks, rolled up my jeans and walked along the edge of the water. There was a flat white rock just a couple of feet from the bank. I sat down there and looked around. The water was gray-green, sliding slowly by like a ribbon. There was a long island in the middle of the river, covered with scrub brush and trees. A few crows were having an argument. Sometimes farmers took their cattle out there by barge and left them for the summer. Cows don't like to swim.

I picked a grasshopper out of the bag and shoved the hook up through his behind. The point came out around his neck with a little crunch. We didn't worry too much about their feelings. Grasshoppers devour crops and we spent a small fortune every year trying to kill as many as we could. The hook was about a foot below the cork. There was another seven or eight feet of line to the end of the bamboo pole. I gave the pole a flip. The line, cork and hook with the grasshopper sailed out over my head and plopped into the water. The current pulled the cork downstream until the string angled it over, making a little V in the water. I could hear Jim and Barry arguing about something. There was a series of bumps as a blue pickup drove over the bridge. Otherwise it was quiet. The cork wasn't moving. I closed my eyes and leaned back, enjoying the warm sun on my face and breathing in the smell of clover and sage. And there were Mom and Dad, and we were little kids just learning to swim. Dad was in his bathing suit in the water. He'd cut a bunch of willow branches and was sticking them into the mud, creating a pen where it was safe to swim. The river looked slow and lazy, but underneath the muddy surface it was dangerous. The current continually chewed away at the bank. They were always telling us stories about people who'd disappeared into six-foot holes just a couple of feet from shore or about fishermen who'd drowned with hip waders on because they'd taken one step too many. That's why we stayed in the pen. Dad had us swim from branch to branch. And we measured our progress that way. Mom usually stayed on shore sitting on a blanket. A cousin had drowned when she was little, and her family had been afraid to go swimming after that. I thought it was weird for anyone to be afraid of water.

Suddenly I heard yelling. I jumped up. Jim was looking upstream. A girl appeared around a bend from behind some willows. She was crying and yelling as she ran toward us. I couldn't hear what she was saying. I jumped off the rock and ran through the mud toward her.

The girl stumbled and fell just as she reached Jim. She looked up, shrieking. "He's trying to kill himself. I tried to stop him but he won't listen."

I recognized her. It was Rita from a town up the line. She was fourteen maybe, with short brown hair, scrawny with flowered pedal pushers and a T-shirt. Her mom was divorced.

"Who's trying to kill themselves?" Jim yelled as he helped her up.

"Where?" I yelled, grabbing her by the shoulders.

Barry ran up, whirled toward the bridge and pointed. "Look!" he shouted. "There!"

About a third of the way across the bridge, a man in a black sweatshirt and jeans was standing on top of the guardrail, holding on to a girder.

"Who is it?" Jim asked.

"What the hell's he doing?" asked Barry.

We watched, suddenly afraid. Afraid that if we moved, something bad would happen. And just then, it did. The man jumped.

"Oh shit!" someone said.

The stranger dropped silently, like a store window dummy, with his arms stretched out to the sides, legs together. It seemed to take a long time. Then finally—a huge splash. And he disappeared.

Fear flushed through me like poison. I wanted to run away. Barry and Jim were staring out at the water. Rita was shrieking. We stood there, waiting for the guy to appear, hoping he'd just come up and wave and start swimming for shore.

There was a small sandbar downstream from the bridge, this side of the island. Maybe I could catch the guy if the current took him there. Quickly I unbuckled my belt and pulled off my jeans.

"What are you doing?" asked Jim, his eyes big.

"I've got to get him or the current will sweep him away. Barry! Rita! Run up and get help. Stop a car." I whipped off my sweatshirt but left my T-shirt on.

"Jim, spot for me." I ran into the water, took a breath and dove in.

When I came up, Jim was yelling. "There he is!"

I saw the guy's head, still upstream from me, and then he was gone. Jim yelled again, "He's pushing himself under! Stop, you bastard!"

The guy was about a hundred feet away. I put my head down and swam. I thought of Dad and how he could cut through the water like a submarine, his hands slicing into the water with hardly a splash. I heard Dad saying, "Keep your fingers together, cup your hands slightly. Pull! Pull!"

I couldn't see a thing in the muddy water. I looked back at shore. Jim pointed right at me. "Behind you," he yelled.

There was a gray shadow in the water a few yards away. *Shit. I can't believe this.* I thought of the drills I'd learned in swimming lessons. *Approach from behind. Grab him by the chin, keep his head out of the water, do a sidestroke and scissor kick to shore.*

I could die here! I thought, surprised as much as afraid. I took a few more strokes and bumped into his body. He was floating face down, a few inches below the surface. I grabbed his sweatshirt.

"Got him!" I yelled. Jim was walking along the bank and I realized the current was sweeping us past the sandbar. I tried to turn the guy over, to get his face out of the water, but he was too heavy. I started pulling him toward shore, kicking hard, stroking with my free arm as hard as I could.

Dammit. He's going to drown. I stopped, tried to turn him again, but he just rolled over.

Dad and I had water-skied right here this summer. We always tried to dump each other. He'd circled our boat around and, when I was far out to the side and going as fast as I could, he took me over a huge wake. I wiped out. We were both laughing as he came up in the boat while I lay back in the water waiting for the ski rope. "You look like you were born in that water." It was the nicest thing he'd ever said to me.

"Swim! Swim!" Jim yelled from shore.

I was swimming for all I was worth. My arms ached. I was angry for not being better, stronger. I was angry at my swimming instructors for making rescues sound easy.

"You're close," yelled Jim. "Keep going." Another couple of strokes and the end of my fishing pole was in front of me. I grabbed it.

"Hang on," yelled Jim. He pulled on the pole until I touched bottom just a few feet from the bank.

Jim ran into the water. He grabbed one of the guy's arms and threw it over his shoulder. I grabbed the other. We stumbled and fell and crawled ashore. We dragged the guy through the mud, rolled him over onto his back on the stones and lay there for a second gasping like goldeye.

For the first time I saw his face. He was green. I knelt beside him, pulled his head back, opened his eyelids and looked into his eyes. They were brown and his pupils were big black dots. The man had puked. There were chunks of food and yellow foam around his mouth. I bent down, put my mouth on his and started blowing. We'd seen a first aid film in high school, but I didn't know what I was doing. Desperately I just blew.

Jim dropped down beside us. The puke got to me. Between breaths I turned to the side and retched, but nothing came up. More breaths. I slapped the man on the face. "Come on, buddy. Come on." I took more breaths. It seemed like a long time. I looked up at Jim.

"Where the hell is help? What happened to Barry? Where are the cops!" I wished Dad were here. He'd know what to do.

Mom was right. Dad and I didn't talk much. He wasn't happy farming. And he sure didn't want me to farm either. I couldn't blame him. Always looking up at the sky to see if it's going to rain so your year's work doesn't go to waste. Too many times it didn't. And the crops just burnt up and our hopes went with them. I think that's why Dad liked the river so much. He was happiest down here. We all were. It was the water; it made things green and alive.

There was no sign of life in the man. Jim got up, walked a few steps and barfed. I continued to blow, then retch, then blow. The man's face was now blue.

You're supposed to wake up and start coughing and spitting, I thought. "Come on, guy."

The siren was a beautiful sound. In a couple of minutes, two RCMP cops ran up. They knelt in the mud, one on each side, and took over. One looked at me. "You know him?" I shook my head.

"How long was he in there?"

"I don't know," I said, looking at Jim. "Seven, eight minutes maybe."

"At least that," said Jim.

The cop looked down, his face grim. I sat on a rock. Barry was there. He had my clothes. I pulled off my wet T-shirt and put on my sweatshirt, still too shocked to be cold. I looked closely at the man for the first time. He was twenty maybe; it was hard to tell. He had new jeans, a nice leather belt, new running shoes, a good sweatshirt. Not the clothes of someone poor or depressed. His skin was dark though and he had long black hair. *Indian. Poor bastard.*

One of the fences in our summer pasture ran by three Indian tepee rings. They were perfect circles of rocks used to hold down the deerskin tents. The rocks were half-buried in the prairie now, covered in rust and yellow lichen. Dad and I would sit there, sweaty and brown, on that grassy hilltop looking down to the river. The shadows of clouds raced over the hills, and I imagined braves in buckskin racing bareback. And there in the quiet, with the breeze whispering through foxtail grass, I felt like one of them. And here was an Indian laying blue and dead. *If they don't get the cancer, this could be Dad.*

There was a sudden crashing in the willows and four men from town came running with a stretcher. Volunteer firemen. We lifted the guy onto the stretcher. "We've got Mel's station wagon," one said to the cops. "Doc Drummond's on his way. He'll meet us in town."

They carried the stranger away, their faces hard. Jim, Barry and I followed them up the bank. They loaded the guy into the back of a dusty Chrysler. One cop got in and kept working on him. The rear door closed and the car roared away, spraying gravel and dust.

He's dead.

Rita was sobbing. "I'm so sorry I couldn't stop him. I felt so helpless." Her pants had a dark spot where she'd peed herself.

A small crowd had arrived, people who'd heard the fire
bell ring in town and followed the truck down for a look.
"What happened?" said a pretty woman in a flowery dress.
"Who was it?"

"Was he from here?" asked a sunburnt cowboy.

Barry, Jim and I went over to the car. We got in and just
sat for a moment. My feet and legs were scratched and
bleeding and covered with mud. So were Jim's. We drove up
the winding hill road, taking the back route home. No one
said anything for a long time.

"What a way to die," Jim said. "We don't even know his
name."

We drove the rest of the way in silence. I went upstairs,
changed into dry clothes and brushed my teeth for a long
time. It was weird to have a dead man's vomit in my mouth.
Jim and Barry were sitting on the porch steps. I gave Jim
some dry sweats and went into the basement and got a bottle of beer. It was covered with dust, probably left over from
Christmas. Dad didn't drink much.

I handed the bottle to Jim. "I don't think Dad will
mind. Got to get this damn taste out of my mouth."

The three of us sat there on the steps, passing the beer
back and forth, staring out toward the barn. It looked different somehow, brighter, like it had been repainted. The
trees were different, too. I'd never noticed how beautiful
bare branches looked, all tangled together like that. The
river had changed, too. It wasn't just fishing and fun and stories anymore. Now a stranger's body would be there just
below the surface. His blue face a part of the shore. I
watched a rivulet of white foam run down the neck of the
bottle, down through the picture of a train, across a wheat
field and grain elevator. *Mom's wrong about Dad and me. I do
care.* Down in the basement there was one dusty bottle of
beer left. I'd saved it for him.

Saying Good-bye to the Tall Man

THE WEATHER-BEATEN DOOR rolled open with the usual protest—rusty metal wheels screeching on the metal track. I stepped over the worn wooden sill and into the dark coolness of the barn. A long sigh. It felt safe here. Maybe the darkness would erase things, maybe even the day itself.

I slid the door shut. To my right an enclosed wooden stairway led up to the loft. The steps were covered with dust and straw. I sat down on one. The big trapdoor above was closed. There was a light switch by my head on the wall, but the quiet of the dark was better. In this gloomy cave I inhaled the comforting smells of old dust, harness, ropes, hay and cows. On the wall beside me there was faded writing in pencil. I couldn't see it in the dark but traced my fingers over the boards, reading the silvered grain like Braille. Grandpa had shown it to me years ago. I knew it by heart.

> Barn erected July 16, 1914
> Sunny, hot, 17 people here
> Ted

Ted was my Grandpa, my dad's dad. He was tall and thin, straight as a telephone pole. Swallows could build nests under the big bushy eaves of his eyebrows. He had blue eyes that glistened like stones in a riverbank pool. And thick white hair that always looked like he'd combed it with a rake. Mom called it "touseldy." But mostly Grandpa wore a white Stetson with a flat brim, and when he walked toward me, with his big white hat and his big white teeth, I knew he was happy to see me. Not like today.

I couldn't breathe. A noose tightened around my neck. Standing up I yanked on the knot of my tie, tore open the top of my Sunday shirt. I felt the button release, heard the tiny sound of it landing. But it was gone—disappeared into some secret dusty place. I wiped off the seat of my good pants and walked into the shop, in a converted stall right next to the stairs.

Dad's shop was in our new machine shed. This place, with its old tools and old cobwebs, was always Grandpa's. I just stood there. Everything was covered with a velvety mouse-brown layer of dust, including the window above the bench. A few rays of light struggled through; specks of dust hung in the beams like stars.

Everything looked strange, like I'd never seen it before. The walls bristled with stuff hanging on nails: old truck fan belts, Swedish crosscut saws, braces and bits, pieces of metal chain, harness buckles, a horse bridle, draw knife, hacksaws, rusty handsaws, tin dust goggles with cracked yellow glass lenses, hand-carved wooden airplane propellers and a faded picture from a 1952 calendar of a green Ford driving down a treelined lane.

Grandpa had built shelves between the upright two-by-fours on the walls. Every shelf was jammed with old card-board boxes and tin cans half-full of cotter keys and cotter pins, screws of all sizes, shiny ball bearings wrapped in oily paper, washers, connecting links for chains. He'd built the wooden workbench of heavy planks, now black with oil and dirt. In the middle was a big iron vice, nicked and dimpled from years of hammering. I'd made many of the marks myself. To the right a hand-operated grinding wheel for sharpening knives and chisels. It whined like a jet engine when we kids wound it up to a hundred miles an hour.

I stood in front of the hand-operated drill press mounted on the wall. Its wooden handle glowed with years of oil from oily hands. Its gears purred as they turned slowly. I'd drilled a lot of holes here—making boats or slingshots or wooden guns. I imagined Grandpa standing on this spot, hunched over some broken piece of machinery, anxious to get back out to the field, back to the horses and the hired men, and back to his work. I leaned my forehead against the cold steel adjusting wheel at the top of the drill. My body heaved like a dog trying to hork up breakfast. But nothing happened. I wasn't very good at crying.

Grandpa's dead! I kicked a wooden box; black bolts skittered across the floor like mice. He'd had a heart attack last week. Two days later he was gone. Grandma had died three years ago. They'd never come out from town for visits again. They'd never drive up our lane slowly in their old blue Chev. Grandpa used to get out, stretch his arms, turn to me and say, "Let's go have a look around." Grandma would go into the house or down to the garden with Mom, and Grandpa and I'd walk around the farm so he could see what Dad was up to. How the buildings and machinery looked. The fences Dad had fixed. The mowing I'd done. We'd check out the chickens, the new litter of pigs. And sample the rhubarb growing in the hollow by the pasture fence.

We always ended up in the barn, out of the heat and the wind. He'd sit on an old milk stool—a section of tree with a leather handle nailed to it; the top polished smooth by farmers' butts—and he'd tell me stories. He'd talk about coming to Saskatchewan from the States with his brother in 1903.

"The only thing here was a stake in the ground, a survey stake with a number on it." He'd chew on a soft green stem of crested wheat grass. "It marked the corner of our 160 acres. Nothing else around for miles but grass and wild flowers. Maybe a meadowlark sitting on the odd stick of a tree. On the horizon you could see one or two of our neighbors' new barns rising up like ships at sea."

Grandpa and his brother had been sodbusters; they'd started their farms side by side and both got married. Grandpa'd married Katarina, who'd come from Austria. They'd called their homestead Bonnieview Farm and painted the name on the barn's big hay door with two crossed Union Jacks underneath. The name and the flags are still there. Sometimes, when the sun was setting and it lit up the barn with an orange light, Grandpa and I would sit on the steps of the house and look at those flags.

We keep only a handful of cows now, but Grandpa talked about when the barn had been full of milk cows, full of their low moo's and soft chewing sounds. "I can still hear the kerosene lantern sliding along the wire in the barn," he said one time. I thought it strange that such a little sound seemed so important to him. He talked about the shadows, too, the way they swayed as the lantern slowly swung while the boys—Dad and my uncles—milked and talked and sang songs to the cows.

"Not one of them could carry a note. With all that awful crooning and warbling going on, I'm surprised those cows didn't produce cottage cheese." Grandpa's eyes would crinkle up and he'd laugh in that quiet way of his.

Grandpa had kept the horses in the barn's lean-to, one team in each stall. Their harness hung on the barn posts beside them. In winter, when it was forty below, there'd be hoarfrost bristling like sugary icicles on the harness buckles. "Those kids just couldn't resist trying to lick it off, and every winter someone's tongue would get stuck to the cold metal. I'd run to the house and get Grandma to heat the kettle and then run back out and pour hot water on the metal to get them unstuck. They always left a little blood and skin behind."

Upstairs in the loft, not much had changed. Grandpa used to put up mountains of fresh loose hay cut from sloughs. We put up our hay in bales now. We'd look up there anyway, stopping to listen to the low conversations of pigeons in the cupola. "Do you think they're the grandchildren of the pigeons that were here when you lived here?" I asked him once.

He had nodded his head. "Oh, without a doubt." That made me feel good.

Grandpa always carried a pencil in his pocket, and whenever he was milking cows, fixing machinery or just resting up after a day of work, he'd stop, take out his pencil and write something on the wall of the barn. It was a habit he got into, and over the years the barn walls filled up with his little notes. On the wall in front of me, above the drill press, beside the holes drilled into the wooden post where the drill bits were kept, he had written another of his messages:

July 17, 1935
Hauling wheat. Grasshoppers bad!
92 in the shade.
Ted

Outside, a crow cawed. A car crunched up the lane. Then another. I heard them stop. I imagined dust hanging behind them like jet trails. A door creaked open—and slammed shut. Half-ton. Then quiet. Just the liquid song of a robin, a few lazy notes from a sun-warmed cricket, the dry whir of a grasshopper flying. Then people talking quietly. Words tumbling, muffled, like a distant stream. Someone laughed! *How can they laugh, for crying out loud? He's dead!* I couldn't go out there. I couldn't face those church-step smiles, the perfumed hugs, the awkward handshakes. I'd had enough of them already today.

A barn cat appeared like a ghost and rubbed against my leg. "Hi there, Bandit." He arched his back and purred loudly as I stroked his long grey fur. Mom used to cut my hair, always used to just chop it off in a brush cut. Until one time when we were visiting Grandma and Grandpa in town and Dad said I needed a haircut. I had started to argue about it when Grandpa turned to Dad and said, "Let the boy grow his hair." No grown-up had ever stuck up for me before. From then on I kept my hair just the way I wanted.

When Grandma died I'd had the mumps and was sick in bed. So I'd never seen someone I knew dead before. Judy Davies, the town undertaker's daughter, had told me what her dad does to bodies. How he takes out their organs and sews up their chests. And then puts felt under their shirts so people can't feel the baseball stitches. There was no way I was going to touch Grandpa. Even though he had his arms folded over his chest and was holding his reading glasses in one hand.

They'd put makeup on him. You could see the smudges of powder around his hair. Reminded me of Aunt Gertie my parents used to have over at Christmas. Grandpa looked like an old doll sleeping in a box. It was scary to look at him. I wished he'd open his eyes and smile and say, "Hey there, sonny boy, how about a little walk?"

Grandpa and Grandma lived in town, but they loved the country. They always carried a wicker picnic basket and a red tartan blanket in their car. They'd pack a thermos of coffee and sandwiches and go on long Sunday drives, just looking at the crops. At harvest time Dad would be combining, a cloud of dust on the horizon. I'd be in the truck, waiting for the hopper to fill up with wheat. And at lunch Grandpa and Grandma's car would appear. Mom would arrive, too, with my sisters and a car full of smells: a big Dutch oven with hot roast beef, with corn on the cob and new potatoes and fresh peas and carrots from the garden. Grandma would help spread the old quilts on the stubble beside the cars.

Grandpa and I'd wander out into the swath. He'd bend over and grab some wheat, break off a few big heads and grind them between his palms. Then he'd hold them close to his mouth and blow the husks and chaff away. He'd peer at the gold kernels in his deeply lined palm like the watch repairman at Eaton's, poke them with his bony finger, check for color, see how fat or shriveled they were. "What do you think?" I knew it was a test.

"Number One," I'd say. And he'd smile, pop the wheat into his mouth and chew to see how hard and dry it was. I followed each step, threw the wheat into my mouth but didn't swallow. I kept chewing until it turned into gum, just like he'd showed me one time, until Dad came round with the combine and it was time to eat.

The meals were feasts. And while we ate, Grandpa and Grandma would hear all the news from my sisters and me. What we'd been doing, where we'd been fishing, whether we were looking forward to school. After pie and coffee, Dad would say good-bye and start up. Mom would clean up, then take my sisters off to a slough to look for frogs. Grandpa and Grandma would lie down in the shade beside the car tire, Grandma with her head on Grandpa's chest and they'd have a snooze. "Just forty winks," Grandpa would say.

More cars were coming up the lane. More people. More words. The ache in my gut wasn't going away. It just sat there like red coals. I still didn't want to go out there.

An old aluminum milk pail hung from an iron hook on a rafter. Cobwebs draped over the handle like lace, the bottom dented where a cow had stepped in it. Instantly I saw Grandpa with the pail tied to his belt, wading into a chokecherry patch in some coulee. The trees were black with berries. The sun was hot. It was quiet, just the odd bee buzzing, the rustling of branches as we milked clumps of berries into the pail, the plip-plip-plip of berries hitting the bottom when the pail was empty; the quieter plopping sounds as it filled up. Sometimes we'd talk. Sometimes the conversation would slow to a trickle, just the odd word passed back and forth in a conspiracy, a comment, a laugh. Often there was just silence.

> *3-day blizzard*
> *-35. Drifts over garage.*
> *Jan 11/29*
> *Ted*

"Want some tea, Kat?" Grandpa'd stand over Grandma as she sat in her recliner. Her arthritis was bad and the chair had heating pads and a vibrator built right into it. Outside it was blizzarding again. I'd stayed in town after school for hockey practice, but now it was storming too hard to get home to the farm. Coming to Grandpa and Grandma's was always the reward you got for being stuck in town. Grandpa'd make potato pancakes with hash and canned peas and corn. I'd watch as he poured the tea in the kitchen. Dad and Mom used to laugh about it. He always held the pot so far from the teacup you never thought the tea would make it. But somehow it arced across the distance and into the cup before gravity knew what was up.

Sometimes an uncle or older cousin would be storm-stayed, too. I'd listen to their conversations—about politics, about the news. After everyone got all talked out, we'd sit in the living room and Grandpa would turn on the radio and

Grandma would turn out the lights. The radio was brown wood with a cloth cover over the speaker and was set into an alcove by Grandpa's chair. In the dark the numbers on the dial glowed. I was drawn to that light like a moth, hungry for stories of the world beyond Saskatchewan. We listened to the CBC, to classical music, which was boring, to radio plays and, best of all, mysteries. I often woke up the next morning on the couch where I'd fallen asleep in my pajamas. Grandpa and Grandma would have put a comforter over me and given me a pillow with a picture of a wolf howling at the moon and the words *Waskesiu, Prince Albert National Park* on it.

I walked out of the shop, over to the old sleigh that was wedged into one of the stalls. It had been there as long as I could remember. I'd never seen it outside the barn. It was an enclosed horse-drawn sleigh. A big yellow plywood box on wood and steel runners. Inside there were two old seats stuffed with horsehair. The windshield was two plate glass windows, and there were two round holes beneath it for the reins to the horses to pass through. Grandpa said they'd had a kerosene heater and buffalo robes and cowhides to keep them warm.

"We'd hook up old Queen and Bess and go across the fields to neighbors to play cards, have a big feed and maybe a singsong around the piano. Later the horses would follow their own tracks home again right to the barn. You could hear the harness bells jingling for a mile in the cold air. And the stars would be so bright and your Grandma would be singing—" Grandpa stopped and I wondered what he was thinking of, and if it was possible at his age to still be in love. And if he missed his old friends and neighbors who were now dying off.

In church today it felt like everyone was looking at me just waiting to see if I was going to cry. Dad didn't. None of

my uncles did, but my aunts sure did. So did Mom especially. She loved Grandpa best of all, I think. We were always stopping in at their house, bringing baking, fresh-cooked meals
that Grandpa could just freeze and then pop into the oven.
Last time we were there, though, I noticed Grandpa had had
an accident going to the bathroom and his pants were a mess,
even his hands. Mom and Dad whispered about it in the car
on the way home. We were all pretty sad. But old Grandpa,
he still stood straight as an arrow, and he still loved to throw
back his head and laugh. When he had his heart attack a few
days ago, my uncles were there within minutes to take him to
the hospital in Riverside. As they were carrying him out he
looked up at George and said, "Well, I guess this is it." Grandpa knew he wasn't coming home again.

The cemetery is just outside of town past the elevators —
a square acre of grass surrounded by tall poplars on the edge
of a field that had just been combined. Grandpa's grave was
right next to Grandma's. The headstone on his side was
empty. Gunnar, Sigurd, Rudy, Axle, Pat and Johnny were pall-
bearers, all farmers. Slowly they pulled the coffin out of the
long black Cadillac that had come from Saskatoon. With big
hands and weathered faces, these friends carried Grandpa to
his grave. Axle stumbled and the coffin tilted. I wondered if
Grandpa's body was rolling inside. I wondered if Grandpa was
watching from somewhere. I wondered what he thought.

The men set the coffin down on two canvas straps
stretched across the black hole. It was neat and tidy and
awful. They were going to put Grandpa down there! In all
that dirt. That's where he'd be until the coffin rotted and his
bones turned to dust. My teeth were clenched like a vice.
My tie was choking me. A puff of wind brought perfume
and aftershave, stubble field, fresh-cut grass and dirt. Someone cleared their throat. Someone sobbed. The minister, a
gray-haired Dutchman, was a friend of Grandpa's and

Grandma's even though they didn't go to church. He stood in his long black robe by Grandpa's head, the elevators in the distance behind him, and he smiled. "This is a day to celebrate life," he said. "A man that loved and was loved by his family and his community." I bit down on my tongue. I stared hard at the orange lilies on top of the coffin.

There was a prayer and then the minister grabbed a handful of dirt and sprinkled it on Grandpa's coffin. And then he shook hands with Dad and Mom and my aunts and uncles. People started talking again quietly. Shaking hands. Hugs. Smiles. It was over. My sisters and I didn't know what to do, so we got into the back seat of our car and waited. Mom and Dad finally got in, looking gray and grim. As Dad started the car I turned and looked out the back window. Mr. Davies, the undertaker, bent over and released something holding the straps. Grandpa's casket started going down, smoothly, like a car on a hoist. In seconds he and the lilies were gone. A breeze sprang up as we drove out; poplar leaves clattered like applause—for Grandpa with his glasses in his hand, in his blue pinstripe suit, with formaldehyde in his veins.

> *Picnicked today in Beaton Coulee*
> *2 inches of rain last night. Crops look good.*
> *Ted & Kat June 30, 1947*

Someone was at the door. It rolled open a bit. A footstep on the cement floor. "You in there?" It was Mom.

"Yeah, in here." I straightened and turned to face her. It was strange to see Mom in the barn, especially in her good church dress and with lipstick on.

"Hi," she said, scanning my face with radar eyes. "You okay?"

I shook my head. And then it happened. All the feelings that had been bottled inside me for the last week, the last three days, welled up like water in a cistern pump. A piston started moving inside my chest, heaving up and down, shaking my shoulders, building up pressure. I stood there, fists clenched at my side, and finally the tears came.

Mom put her arms around me. "I know," she whispered. "I . . ." She stopped, waited, tried to say something but couldn't. Her grip on me tightened. Her shoulders shook. We both stood there crying.

Finally Mom pulled back and looked at me, wiping her eyes. "You know he'll always be right here, don't you?"

Clang. A metallic ring came from outside. "They're playing horseshoes!"

"Yes. Don't you think Grandpa would like that?"

"Yeah, I guess so."

"Well, think you're ready to come out now and say hello?"

"Yeah." I wiped my face and sniffed. "I'll be there in a minute. I have something to do first."

"Okay." Mom moved to the door and stepped out into the light. She stopped and looked up. "Perfect day for a picnic. Bet you that's what they're doing right now." And then she was gone.

I stood there for a minute, then turned and walked back into the shop to the workbench and reached for a can on the shelf. There was the yellow stub of an old carpenter's pencil in it. I looked for a space on the wall.

Edward (Ted) Anderson buried today. Age 92.
All his friends and family here.
Sunny, 78 degrees.
Eric
September 19, 1965